"So why aren't we having sex?" Lee said brightly

Trevor blinked, then looked around the stuffy Manhattan restaurant. "Because we're in the middle of dinner?"

Lee sighed. "I meant why aren't *you* and *I* having sex?"

The words hung in the air. "Um, we're good friends. I didn't know it was an option."

Lee gathered her courage. "Well, who says a person can't have sex with a friend? No strings attached. We're both available." *And I'm half in love with you already....*

The idea of sleeping with Lee had occurred to Trevor before. She was a beautiful woman with all the required female parts in working order. But making love with her?

"I don't know if this is a good idea," he said warily, even as he envisioned her in his bed...wearing something soft and silky.

"We've been friends forever." Lee's heart was racing. *Can't you see how much I care?* "We're comfortable with each other."

Trevor frowned. "Maybe we're comfortable because we *don't* have sex. Maybe having sex would mess everything up."

Suddenly both of them were silent. *It could be a disaster...or dynamite.*

Dear Reader,

What can I say about *Hot and Bothered*? I can tell you it was the most *fun* I've ever had writing a book. Every time I think about the story, I smile and sigh.

Writing a BLAZE is something I've wanted to do ever since these "red-hot reads" came out in Temptation. Nothing's more creative than mixing passion and humor. When I recall the elevator scene and...well, I don't want to spoil it for you!

I received some wonderful news while I was writing about Trevor and Lee—I became a RITA Award finalist for my very first Temptation novel, *One Wicked Night*. Talk about thrilling! To be recognized by the Romance Writers of America for this award left me breathless.

My next book, *Little Girl Lost*, an Intrigue title, will be available in Spring 2000. Then I follow up with another BLAZE for Temptation in the summer. I hope you enjoy my books, and I would love to hear from readers. You can reach me at http://www.joleigh.com.

Best wishes!

Jo Leigh

Books by Jo Leigh

HARLEQUIN TEMPTATION

674—ONE WICKED NIGHT
699—SINGLE SHERIFF SEEKS...
727—TANGLED SHEETS

HEART OF THE WEST

Aug. '99—THE $4.98 DADDY

HOT AND BOTHERED
Jo Leigh

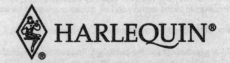

HARLEQUIN®

TORONTO • NEW YORK • LONDON
AMSTERDAM • PARIS • SYDNEY • HAMBURG
STOCKHOLM • ATHENS • TOKYO • MILAN • MADRID
PRAGUE • WARSAW • BUDAPEST • AUCKLAND

To Dianne,
for being my big sister,
and my friend.

ISBN 0-373-25856-9

HOT AND BOTHERED

1

TREVOR TEMPLETON watched as his best friend took a sip of white zinfandel, then put her glass on the table. "So," Lee Phillips said brightly, "why aren't we having sex?"

Trevor blinked, then looked around the somewhat stuffy Manhattan restaurant. "Probably because we're in the No Boffing section. But I'm sure we can change tables."

Lee sighed. "Not right now, for heaven's sake. I mean in general."

Trevor blinked again. Lee always had a tendency to surprise him, but this was unexpected, even for her. "I think we're not having sex because neither of us has a significant other. Or am I missing something?"

"That's not what I meant."

"Okay."

She shook her head as if he were a particularly dull child. "I meant why aren't *you* and *I* having sex?"

The sentence hung in the air like a cartoon bubble. For a moment, he forgot how to breathe. Someone dropped a glass, and he jumped, turning automatically to check out the damage. When he turned back to Lee, she wasn't grinning. She had her serious face on. This wasn't a joke. "First," he said, trying to think logically when everything in him screamed *run*, "I have to know if this is rhetorical. 'Cause if it's not, that's a whole different set of answers."

She gave him a stare, one with her brows furrowed. "No. It's not rhetorical."

He waited a second.

"Yes." She sighed. "It could be."

She still wasn't through. He could tell by the way she nibbled on her lower lip. After eight years, he'd come to recognize the signs. "I'm not sure," she admitted. "Maybe."

"Okay, then. Now that that's clear, I have no idea why we're not having sex. Care to explain this little voyage to the twilight zone?"

Lee picked up her spoon, then put it down again, choosing a sip of wine instead. Considering it was crème brûlée she'd passed on, Trevor knew she was earnest. He debated getting a little cognac, but figured a clear head was called for. As far as friendships went, his with Lee was right up there in the top two. All right, the number one position. But sometimes...

He took a sip of coffee and waited. The explanation would come in its own fashion. Just like always. The trick was not to panic.

"I've been thinking."

"Obviously."

"Don't start."

"I wouldn't dream of it."

"Okay, then. I've been thinking. I'm twenty-seven years old. I've got the career I want. The house I want. I love my cats. I like my privacy. I've always been lousy at love, but as I recall, I was pretty damn good at sex."

"This was an *Oprah* show, wasn't it?"

"You're no spring chicken yourself," she continued, as if he hadn't spoken.

"I'm only six months older than you. Not quite ready to be put out to pasture."

"And you're happy with your life, right?"

"Am I supposed to answer now?"

She nodded.

"Yes," he said. "I'm happy with my life."

"See? So you like where you are, and I like where I am, but neither of us is getting laid. At least I'm not. Are you?"

If he'd been drinking he would have spit across the table. As it was, he just coughed. "I'm sorry, but you must be one of those pod people I'm always reading so much about. Who take over the bodies of innocent stockbrokers when they sleep. When will Lee be coming back?"

"Just answer me."

He shook his head. It was no use fighting. It never was with Lee. "No, dear. I'm not getting laid, as you so delicately put it."

"As if you've never heard the expression."

"I try to use it judiciously."

"Oh, like when you're out with the boys playing poker?"

"Boys? What boys? Do I have boys?"

"Stop confusing things."

"Me?"

"Come on, Trevor. I'm serious."

"You'd better be."

"So why aren't we having sex?" She didn't even crack a smile. "With each other, I mean?"

He felt the need to wipe his brow, but he resisted. "Um, I didn't know it was an option."

"You're not attracted to me, is that it?"

"I didn't say that."

"Well, are you?"

"Jeez, Lee. Show some mercy."

"If we can't be honest with each other after all these years, then what's the point?"

"Honesty is one thing. This is something out of Kafka."

"Just tell me."

He studied her dark brown eyes, her full pink lips, and the way she tucked her hair behind her ears, and realized he'd memorized her face through the years. It was more familiar to him in some ways than his own. "Yes, I'm attracted to you. Happy now?" Trevor racked his brain, trying to figure out what had brought this on. Maybe the date she'd had on Friday? According to her play-by-play, nothing much had happened. She'd thought the guy was nice, but no bells and whistles.

Maybe the gang had gotten to her. Katy, who couldn't help giving advice, especially since all she seemed to do was read self-help books. Or Ben,

Katy's husband, who didn't offer all that much advice, but felt the need to fix Lee up on blind dates. It could have been Susan, but that seemed doubtful. She'd sworn off men since her divorce. Last but not least, it could have been Peter, the one guy in the group who was more of a romantic than Lee herself.

On the other hand, the overall insanity of the idea was right up Lee's alley.

"You're not just saying that to be polite?" Lee asked.

"Saying what?"

Lee shook her spoon at him, flinging a tiny piece of gooey crème brûlée across the table. "You said you were attracted to me. I asked if you said it to be polite."

He laughed. Really laughed. "Polite? With you? You wouldn't know polite if it came up and bit you on the butt."

"Okay, then. That's good. I'm attracted to you, too."

Whoa. He hadn't expected that. A rush of pleasure hit him square in the solar plexus. She was attracted to him? Why should that matter? What in hell was going on here? Who was this woman? "Can we slow down a little? I'd like to try to get my footing on the Tilt-A-Whirl that is your life."

She nodded, then took a big bite of her dessert as if this conversation wasn't the single weirdest in the history of their relationship. "Sure. I'm just saying...it doesn't really make sense, does it? That we should both be living like nuns? There's nothing that says a person can't have sex with a friend, right? You know. No strings attached. We'd just be friends like always."

"Only we'd share underwear secrets?"

"Yeah."

"And body parts."

"Well, we wouldn't exchange them. But maybe they could mingle."

"Uh-huh." She really had him confused. He'd known Lee since freshman year at NYU. He'd been by her side through three really terrible relationships. He was the guy she turned to when things went sour. She'd been there for him, too.

There was no one in the world he cared about more than Lee and the rest of the gang who'd been along for the ride since day one at college, Katy, Ben, Susan and Peter. The six of them were thick as thieves. They'd told each other the most intimate details. His friends were the great joy in his life. Sounding boards, confidants, people who would call him on his bull. But Lee, she was special. She was his rock. Now she wanted to change all that? It didn't make sense.

She frowned. "You don't sound enthusiastic."

"Maybe that's because I've lost the power of coherent thought."

"Why?"

"Oh, no reason," he said, as more oxygen-rich blood left his brain and migrated south. "Is this about babies? Is your biological clock reaching midnight or something?"

She studied him for a moment, thinking. "No. At least I don't think so. I haven't had any baby dreams or anything. I think this is just about sex."

"Well, then. Okay."

"So what do you think?"

He took a sip of coffee. She *was* serious, that much he could tell. She was also insane, but that was neither here nor there. She wanted an answer, and for the life of him, he couldn't think of one.

The idea of sleeping with Lee had occurred to him before, of course. He wasn't blind. She was a beautiful woman with all the required female parts in working order. But having sex with her? Naked?

"Well?"

"I don't know," he said, finally. "I hadn't really considered it."

"Honestly? You've never thought about it? Even once?"

"Of course I've thought about it. But we're friends."

"Exactly."

"Friends as in buddies. Pals. Compadres."

"I've thought about it."

He sat up a little straighter. "Oh?"

She nodded. A small wisp of auburn hair came loose from behind her headband and brushed her temple. He almost reached over to tuck it back, but suddenly the move he wouldn't have given a thought to just moments ago seemed rife with sexual innuendo. Now what was he supposed to do? Ignore it? Mention it casually? Jump under the table and cover his head?

"I like you more than any other person on the planet," she said. "I know you. I know your habits and your quirks. I'm comfortable with you everywhere. I think it makes perfect sense."

"Maybe we're comfortable because we don't have sex. Maybe having sex would mess everything up."

"Yeah, I thought about that. There's a possibility it could, but I don't think so."

"Why not?"

"Because we're going into this with our eyes open. It's not like we have to change how we feel about each other. I love you, and I know you love me. Neither one of us wants to mess with that. I don't want to get married, and you don't either. So there wouldn't be any hidden agendas. Look at Ben and Katy. They were friends first."

"They got married after three weeks."

"Okay, so that wasn't a good example."

"I don't know, Lee," he said, shaking his head. "This has all the earmarks of a disaster."

"You said that about us getting season tickets to the Yankees."

"Okay, so that one worked out. This one has a lot more risk involved."

"I don't see why. Either we'll like it, and continue to do it, making both of us a lot less irritable, or we won't like it, and we'll shake hands and go back to what we've got now. What's so risky about that?"

"There's a little detail you're forgetting about. Intimacy. It has a way of changing relationships. Or have you forgotten?"

"This is different," she said, her confidence rock-solid. "I'm already intimate with you."

"No, you're not."

"Do I or do I not shower at your house every Sunday morning?"

"Yes, but I don't wash your back. Besides, that's not the kind of intimacy I'm talking about."

"Oh, you mean emotional intimacy."

"Uh-huh. The kind that hurts. You remember."

A shadow of pain darkened her eyes, and he twisted the napkin in his lap. He knew where her ex-boyfriend lived. Lee would never know if he paid the bastard a little visit.

She firmed her lips. "I don't think that's going to be an issue."

"You don't?"

She shook her head. "Nope. I love you. But I'm not 'in love' with you. Having sex won't change that."

"How do you figure?"

"Let me ask you something. Have you been emotionally intimate with every woman you've slept with?"

"Sure."

"Liar."

"Hey!" he said, wounded that she would even think such a thing.

"I know you haven't. Remember Sandy what's-her-name? From Teaneck? You didn't even like her much. And there was that blonde with the eyebrows.

You told me yourself that all there was between you was sex."

"Granted. But they were exceptions," he said primly.

"So, I'll be one, too."

"They weren't my best friend."

"Which will make me an exceptional exception. We can have it all. Best friends and bed partners. It's simplicity itself. The only way we can muck it up is if we don't tell the truth, which I know we will because we've always told each other the truth."

He released his strangled napkin and reached for his coffee. "I don't know. I'm pretty happy with the way things are right now."

"I'm not unhappy." She signaled the waiter to bring her some coffee. As soon as he was gone, she opened two packs of artificial sugar and emptied them into her cup. "I guess I've been feeling a little..."

"Horny?"

She laughed. "That, too. But that's not all. I'm not lonely—I swear I'm not. I really do love my life just as it is. But it's like that baby monkey and the towel doll."

"Oh, that. I was wondering when you'd bring that up," he said, hoping she'd catch the sarcasm. She didn't, of course. There was some synapse in her head that made baby monkeys relevant to their conversation, but that synapse was unique to Lee.

She sighed at him. "That *National Geographic* special we saw. With the baby monkey who didn't have a mother, so he bonded with the doll they made out of a towel?"

"I remember the documentary, but I don't see the connection."

"I think I need to do a little bonding. And I'd prefer to do it with a friend instead of a towel."

"Imagine how pleased I am not to be considered one step above a towel in your life."

"Knock it off. You know what I'm saying."

"Sort of a surrogate lover kind of thing?"

"Exactly." She smiled. It was her best one, where her eyes crinkled up and her dimple showed. "So, will you think about it?"

"I doubt I'll think of anything else for the rest of my life."

"You're so cute when you're confused."

"I'm glad I can please you."

She bent down and retrieved her purse from under her chair. "It's your turn to pick up the check."

"That's it? Conversation over?"

She nodded. "You need time to think about it. So do I."

"Is there a deadline for this decision?"

"No. Take your time. Whenever you're ready, we can pick it up again. No pressure."

"Thanks."

"Hey, what are friends for?"

"I'm not sure anymore."

She reached over and took his hand in hers. "If it comes down to sex or friendship, the friendship wins, got it?"

He nodded as his gaze moved down to their entwined fingers. God, she had slender fingers. Slender and long, with tapered oval nails. He could practically feel those nails on his back. He had the sinking sensation that despite her conviction, between sex and friendship, friendship didn't stand a chance.

"DID YOU KNOW that a couple in Phoenix went to court to get joint custody of an iguana?"

"That's thrilling, Susan," Lee said. "Honest. If you'd like to talk about reptiles, we certainly can."

"Oh! Oh, God. I forgot! Did you do it?"

Lee curled her feet under her and checked to make sure her cup of cappuccino was within reach. She leaned back in her leather club chair, really pleased with the way her new halogen lamp gave off such wonderful diffused light. It made her couch look better, her bookcases more interesting, and it hid all the dust bunnies. She adjusted her phone on her shoulder. "I did indeed."

"And?"

"He was surprised."

"Well, duh. But what did he *say?*"

"He said he'd think about it."

"I can't stand it. How did you bring it up?"

Lee heard a muffled electronic baritone voice in the background telling Susan that she had mail. Lee pictured Susan exactly—lying on her antique four-poster bed, bolstered by an amazing array of pillows, laptop where it was designed to sit, fuzzy slippers dangling off her toes. The television was probably on, too, and last but not least, the *New York Times* was undoubtedly spread around her body like a cape.

"I asked him over coffee."

"Just like that?" Susan asked, her voice almost an octave higher.

"Uh-huh."

"Oh, God, Lee you're amazing. What did he say?"

"He's worried that it'll ruin the friendship."

"Did you tell him you only want him for his body?"

"Susan. I don't. I think we can go that extra step, that's all."

"Honey, I think it's the smartest thing since caller ID. This way, you can stop going out on all those ridiculous fishing expeditions."

"Fishing? They're called dates."

"I went on a date once. Look what happened to me."

"Susan, just because Larry turned out to be The Jerk with No Conscience, it doesn't mean that every relationship ends up in disaster. Look at Katy and Ben."

"Katy and Ben are inexplicable. My theory is that they both saved hundreds of children in a past life, and therefore are being rewarded in this one. I, on the other hand, must have kicked puppies for a living."

"Susan, you have a wonderful life."

"Just because I inherited money, doesn't mean everything's hunky-dory."

"No, but it's better than a poke in the eye with a sharp stick."

"Yeah, yeah," Susan said, brushing off the familiar litany.

"Anyway," Lee said, swinging the conversation back around. "You should have seen his face."

"Trevor's?"

"No, the mayor's. Of course, Trevor's. It was great. I thought his jaw would drop in his coffee."

"I should have gone. Worn a disguise or big old coat. I can just see his little panic lights go off."

"That would have been subtle," Lee said, unable to imagine the disgustingly tall and beautiful blond in anything that hid even one of her perfect curves. "Besides, the panic part only lasted a few seconds. Then I think he was pretty okay with it."

"Knowing Trevor, this isn't going to be decided anytime soon."

"Yeah. But I'm in no particular rush. Although, now that it's out there..."

"The rhinoceros on the kitchen table."

"Maybe I should just tell him to forget it. What if we can't get past it? What if the rhinoceros is so big, we lose sight of each other?"

"Give it more than five minutes, will you, Lee?"

"I don't know. It feels—" Lee heard the beep of her call waiting. She knew who it was. "Listen, I think it's Katy on the other line. I'll call you back."

"Okay. We're on for lunch tomorrow?"

"Yeah."

TREVOR CLICKED the mute button on his TV remote when the phone rang. It might be Lee. On the other hand, it might be Ben. On the fifth ring, he picked up. "Hello?"

"Hey, Trevor. How's it going?"

He breathed a small sigh of relief, and settled back in his big chair. "Ben, let me ask you something."

"Okay."

"Are women completely nuts?"

"Yes, Trevor. They are. Just breathe deeply, and let it go. There's nothing you can do about it."

"Okay. I just wanted to make sure."

"Anything specific?"

Trevor debated telling Ben the truth. But Lee was going to tell Katy, so what the hell was he worried about? By tomorrow morning Katy, Ben, Susan and Peter would know everything, right down to what he ate for dinner. Maybe Ben already knew.

"Lee," Trevor said, finally.

"So she really did it, eh? Hey, hold on a minute. The pizza's here."

Trevor groaned. It never changed. Ever since college, the six of them had been like this. Susan itched, Peter scratched. Their lives were so enmeshed that it was a wonder any of them could tie their shoelaces by themselves. Although he and Lee had always been tight, Trevor also felt a close bond to Ben. The only other native Californian, he'd been just as bewildered by New York as Trevor had been when they first got to college. Ben and he had been roommates in the beginning, until Ben had married Katy.

Trevor always smiled when he thought of their wedding. City hall, everyone dressed in jeans, including the bride. He'd almost lost the ring, but found it in his wallet. Katy had cried the whole time, especially when Susan had shown up with a big bouquet of roses for Katy to hold.

And now the friends had become a family of sorts. Trevor was closer to the five of them than he was to his own parents and siblings. It was Ben and Lee, in fact, who had encouraged him to push so hard for his job at the magazine. Being a wine critic at twenty-five was practically unheard of at the time, but his friends had supported him until he snagged the job. Of course, he still had a way to go until he was the *main* critic, but he didn't mind being second banana. At least, not yet.

"I'm back," Ben said, although his voice was a little muffled from all the chewing. "So you were saying that she did it?"

"She did it indeed." Trevor pulled himself back to the conversation. "When did you find out? You could have warned me, you know."

"I didn't hear until tonight. I think Katy knew I would blow the whistle."

"Katy is perceptive."

"For what it's worth, she doesn't think it's such a good idea."

"No?" Trevor's gaze went from the TV to his computer, and he cringed at the work he still had to do tonight. The article on the Merlots was due tomorrow, and his editor didn't have a good sense of humor about tardiness.

"Nope," Ben said. "Not according to the self-help book du jour. Tomorrow, it could change though."

"Hasn't the woman ever heard of fiction?"

Ben laughed. "So, what did you decide to do?"

"Nothing. I panicked."

"I hear that."

"I don't know." Trevor turned his head so he wouldn't have to look at his computer anymore. "It doesn't seem like a good idea to me, either. Except..."

"What?"

"It's Lee, for God's sake."

"I know."

"I've thought about it before," he admitted, wondering briefly if he should just keep his mouth shut.

Ben chuckled. "You wouldn't have been human if you didn't. Personally, I don't know why you didn't jump on her in the dorms. You had your chance, you know."

"I chose the high road."

"You were a big, fat chicken who was so afraid of commitment, you'd hyperventilate if a woman asked you to spend the night."

"That, too," Trevor admitted.

"But honestly, the idea itself has some intriguing aspects."

"For instance?"

"A dream fulfilled. Completing the circle..."

"Has Katy left one of her books in the bathroom?"

"I'm not kidding, Trevor. You'd better think this through. It might be just what the doctor ordered. I mean when's the last time you took a big risk? Besides drinking red wine with fish? Face it, Trevor old boy. Sometimes you need to jump off the cliff, even if you don't know where you're going to land."

Trevor got up, too unnerved to keep still. He walked to the kitchen, still carrying the phone, and got a beer from the fridge. "You and Katy were friends first."

"True."

"And you turned out great."

"Also true. But we didn't try to switch horses midstream. We knew from day one we weren't going to stay just friends."

"Maybe Lee and I are supposed to stay just friends." He headed back to his comfy chair, using his elbow to turn off the kitchen light.

"I might have gotten this wrong, but isn't that what she wants? Just friends, with certain perks?"

Trevor opened the beer, then took a big swig. "Yeah."

"A minefield, my friend. But maybe one worth traversing."

"Well, that's helpful."

Again, Ben laughed. "Katy's on the other line. With Lee."

"I figured."

"So I'll see you Sunday?"

"Yeah."

"Trevor?"

"Yep?"

"Good luck."

"I'm gonna need it." He hung up the phone and flopped into his chair again. CNN was on, but it was entertainment news. His gaze moved to the picture sitting on his set, right next to the cable box. It was the gang. He had his arm around Lee's shoulder.

He leaned back and closed his eyes. It was far too easy to imagine her without her clothes on. In his bed. With those long fingers of hers trailing down his chest. Because he'd imagined it since the day they'd met.

2

LEE LET TREVOR jog ahead of her. Not because she was tired, but because she wanted to look at him. Ever since she'd come up with the idea of adding sex to the relationship, Trevor wasn't just Trevor anymore.

She'd really gotten a jolt this morning when she'd arrived at his place for their Sunday morning run. They'd had the same Sunday agenda for years now. Jog at the park first, then back to his place for a quick shower, breakfast and a leisurely read through the *New York Times*. Lunch at the Broadway Diner with the gang followed. Overnight guests were allowed to come along, but most of the time it was just the six of them. Unless Trevor was traveling. Or Peter was in a play. But mostly, one Sunday was like the next. The routine was as comfortable as an old sweater. At least it used to be.

But today, when he'd opened the door, her first thought had been about sex. It wasn't as if she'd never seen him in his jogging shorts before. Yet this morning, she'd been incredibly aware of his chest. It was a great chest. Broad in the shoulders, narrow at the waist. A nice sprinkling of dark hair for that masculine appeal. He didn't have a six-pack stomach, but he was lean and strong and muscled.

Then she'd noticed his face. A face she'd thought was as familiar to her as her own. But something was different. Her perception had changed, although she really didn't understand why. Trevor had always been good-looking. But that wasn't what was important about him. He could have looked like a frog, and she'd still have loved him. Today, his looks had an impact that took her totally by surprise. It was as if she were seeing him for the first time.

His dark hair, slightly wavy, long over the collar, fit him perfectly. She'd always admired his eyes. They were green, really green. A lot of people thought he wore colored lenses, but she knew better. Those big eyes of his were twenty-twenty. What she didn't understand was why she hadn't noticed his eyelashes before. They were ridiculously long for a man. She should have those lashes, not him.

Then, of course, there was his mouth. His smile had always given her pleasure, but she'd never analyzed why. The guy had one of the top ten mouths she'd ever seen. Perfectly shaped lips over even, white teeth. It was an incredibly kissable mouth. All these years, and she'd been oblivious. Well, except for the first year at NYU. She'd thought about his looks a lot back in college. But they never seemed to be available at the same time, so she'd forced herself not to think about him like that. By the time they were both free and clear, they'd already become friends. Now that she *was* thinking about him like that, it amazed her that it hadn't come up years ago.

Okay, so his nose was a little crooked, and he had that scar on his right temple, but somehow that just added to his charm.

All in all, he was a remarkable specimen. Who would have thought? Had she really taken him for granted all this time? No wonder he was asked out by all sorts of women. Smart, handsome, kind and funny, he was everything a person could want in a friend. And in a lover.

"Hey, what's the matter?"

She stumbled a little at Trevor's words. She'd been so lost in thought that she'd slowed down to a walk. He faced her now, hands on hips, concern furrowing his forehead. "You okay?"

She nodded. "Just woolgathering."

"Well, gather it later. I'd like to finish this run today."

"Oh, keep your shirt on." She started jogging again, and in a second she was at his side, and they fell into their familiar rhythm.

"What was that all about?" he asked.

Lee debated telling him, but decided against it. How was she supposed to admit that she hadn't really looked at him for years? He'd be insulted, and he'd have every right. "Nothing," she said. "Just work."

"Ah," he said. "And here I was, assuming you were lost in thought about me."

"You? Why would I be thinking about you?"

"Because I'm a complex man in a complex world."

"Where'd you read that? *Esquire?*"

"If you must know, it was a fortune cookie."

"Ah."

Trevor picked up the pace a bit, so talking took a back seat to breathing. It didn't take long for her thoughts to go right back to where she'd left off.

Sleeping with Trevor. Seeing him naked. Touching. Kissing. Fondling.

What if he made funny noises? Her last boyfriend had shouted, "Oh, mama," every time he climaxed. By the end, she'd wanted to stuff a sock in his mouth. Of course, she'd wanted to do that even when they weren't in bed. She was still annoyed with herself for staying with Carl so long. He was a first-class jerk, but she hadn't seen that until she'd been living with him for almost a year.

She was grateful to him for one thing. He'd been the catalyst for the revelation that had changed her life. After their ugly breakup, she'd finally seen that she wasn't meant to be in a romantic relationship. She simply wasn't any good at it.

In all other areas of her life, she was competent. She was successful at her job at the brokerage house, particularly with high-tech stock, she had great friendships, and she didn't have any terrible vices. Overall she was proud and content with the way things were. But love? Nope.

She'd come to the conclusion that romantic love was a talent, like painting or having a good voice. Genetic, like blond hair or big feet. It wasn't her fault that she was completely inept. That she picked wildly inappropriate men. That she lost all her good sense as soon as her emotions got involved. It just was. Once she'd accepted that fact, life had fallen into place.

The only problem was that she missed sex...which led her right back to Trevor.

If she couldn't feel safe having sex with Trevor, then something was seriously wrong with the world. He would never hurt her. He would always be considerate. She trusted him completely. And she knew that he was utterly, unalterably antimarriage. He'd told her that many times. His position was fixed, and he had never wavered. Perfect.

So, why was she still so hesitant?

They reached the last turn, and slowed down to a walk. Trevor was a stickler for stretching and cooling, and although she was impatient with the last fifteen minutes, she dutifully went through the paces. More to please him than because she believed it was necessary for her body.

As she watched him sit on the grass and bend low over his right leg, she wondered if she should quit all this pondering and get down to business. The only way to find out if this was going to work was to do it.

They were going back to his apartment in a moment. He always let her have the first shower.

She sat down next to him and spread her legs. Bending over, grabbing her right foot and easing into the stretch, she made up her mind. When it was time to take her shower, she was going to invite him to join her.

TREVOR WAS officially worried. Ever since their conversation the other night, he'd been obsessed with the idea of having sex with Lee. Being with her this morning had not improved the situation. On the contrary, he'd barely been able to run. He kept imagining all sorts of things. Sexy things. Dangerous things. It occurred to him that he'd probably been having these X-rated thoughts about Lee for years, but because there was no point, he'd repressed them. Now that the door had been opened, even just that little crack, his imagination was running wild.

Which, he figured, wasn't exactly what Lee had in mind. She was probably thinking that sex between them would be very polite and civilized.

Now that they were nearly back at his apartment, the severity of his problem was becoming obvious. It was difficult to be subtle in these damn shorts. But every time he tried to think of something safe, baseball scores or his stock portfolio, he'd wind up picturing her in his shower. Wonderful. They hadn't even done anything yet, and he was out of control. God forbid she should bring up the subject. He'd never be able to face her again.

Why had she come up with this stupid idea anyway? Didn't she realize she'd be opening Pandora's box? That once the concept was planted, it couldn't be unplanted? Well, he wouldn't go down without a fight. He valued her friendship too much. But the sex thing, that wasn't going to happen. It couldn't. He couldn't take it.

"Are you going to open the door sometime soon?"

He jerked out of his thoughts, and realized he'd been standing still, staring at his front door for who knows how long. His key was out, and he slipped it in the lock. Lee walked in first.

He, of course, had to check out her rear end. For the fiftieth time this morning. Nothing had changed. It was the same bottom he'd seen the first time. But that didn't seem to matter. He had to look. To admire. To sigh.

"What?" She turned to him, standing there all flushed and tousled and beautiful. Her breasts rising and falling, making it hard not to stare at her like some Central Park pervert. He forced his gaze down her long, lean body, but that only made things worse. He sighed again.

"Trevor?"

"It's nothing."

"Sighing like that usually means you've heard from your mother."

He shook his head. "Nope." He wasn't about to admit what he'd been thinking about. Time for a distraction. "I'll go put on the coffee. You get in the shower."

She hesitated. He didn't. He walked quickly to the safety of the kitchen, where his lower body was hidden behind the counter. That way, no matter what she said, he'd maintain a little dignity.

"Um, Trevor?"

He got the coffee canister from the cupboard. "Yeah?"

"About the shower."

He knew just what she was going to say. She was going to ask him to join her. Oh, damn, what should he do? His body was screaming, "Yes, yes!" but was that wise? If she didn't stop looking at him that way, the wise vote was going to be trounced by the go-for-it vote.

"I, uh...I..."

"What?" He cringed. He hadn't meant to bark at her. She'd even jumped a little.

"Nothing," she said.

"Hey, I didn't mean to be so testy. It's just that..."

"Yes?"

"I'm just hot, is all."

"Oh."

Damn. Had he scared her off? Good. Well, sort of good. It was too easy to imagine himself raising her arms, taking hold of the bottom of her T-shirt, pulling it slowly up past her stomach, then her breasts. Lingering for a moment to admire, to picture what lay beneath the bra, then moving his hands once more until the shirt was off. Tossing it casually to the floor. Meeting her gaze. And then... Oh, God. This was Lee he was thinking about! Lee who'd nursed him through the breakup with Rebecca. Who'd seen him drunk, sick, stupid. The woman he could count on, no matter what. What the hell was he thinking?

She must have been following the same trail of thoughts, because she turned and hurried toward

the shower. He could have stopped her. All he'd
have to do was say her name. But he didn't, and then
she was gone.

He looked down. He'd been scooping coffee into
the pot. A lot of coffee. Shaking his head, he dumped
the whole thing back into the canister and started
again. This time he counted. When he was through,
he filled the carafe with water, then turned the machine on. That's when he heard the shower start.

This was impossible.

He would have to talk to her. Tell her it was a
crazy idea. It risked everything, and to what end?

Moving to the living room, he took the newspaper
out of its plastic bag and started to put it together the
way they liked it. He got the news, the opinion section and the comics first. She got the sports section so
she could catch up on her beloved Yankees, the financial section and the TV guide. The rest was up for
grabs.

He sat down with the front page, but kept it folded
in his lap. The thing was, he knew her so well. How
she got personally affronted when the Yankees lost.
How she stirred her coffee an annoyingly long time
when she was reading. The different sounds of her
laughter. Yet there were still mysteries. What she
looked like when she slept. He'd imagined her body,
but that was just filling in the blanks with other images. She'd be completely unique. Completely beautiful.

Dammit, was he a complete fool? How could he
run from the chance that with Lee he could have ev-

erything? A companion, a friend, a lover. All without the inevitable ugliness that came along with marriage—at least, all the marriages he'd seen. He'd read about the perfectly happy couples who celebrated fifty, sixty years of wedded bliss. But in his experience, that was all myth. Except for Ben and Katy, but they were clearly from another planet, so they didn't count.

His own parents had shown him all he really needed to know about marriage. They'd each been married four times, all unsuccessful. All ugly, bitter and vengeful. No, thank you.

But Lee's proposition wasn't for marriage. It was for something completely different. They wouldn't have a chance to become bored with each other, because they wouldn't live together. She wouldn't depend on him to make her happy. She'd do that on her own. He wouldn't expect her to make his life tidy. That would be his responsibility.

He listened to the shower for a moment. She hadn't finished yet. Maybe it wasn't too late. He put the paper aside and stood. Eyed the long walk to the bathroom. Then his phone rang.

He picked up the receiver, embarrassingly relieved. "Hello?"

"Is she there? Have you done it yet?"

Trevor shook his head as he heard Peter's voice. "Jeez, Peter. Was this on the news or what?"

"Something this big can't be hidden, Trevor. It's way too juicy."

"All of you need to get a life. Or an insurance plan with a big mental health rider."

"So, answer me."

"No."

"No, you won't answer me, or no, you haven't done it?"

"Both."

"Damn. Here I thought someone was going to get lucky today. So much for romance."

"I gather things aren't working out with what's-his-name?"

"Fox. And yes, I saw the actual birth certificate. He decided to go back to Idaho. For the skiing. I mean, I can understand wanting to ski, but, for God's sake, Idaho? I must remember to stick to urbanites."

"If I recall, you told me it was his rural roots that attracted you in the first place." Trevor had known the relationship between Fox and Peter wasn't going to make it. Peter was always hooking up with gorgeous young twinkies, and being disappointed when he discovered that there was nothing inside them but cream filling. Peter might look like them— dark, wavy hair, lean, movie-star handsome—but, inside, Peter was a substantial man. Someone Trevor could lean on. That is, when the actor wasn't in the throes of another shattered love affair.

"I was a fool," Peter said with a sigh. "Blinded by the rip in his jeans."

"I'm sorry it didn't work out."

"Me, too. Oh well, *c'est la vie*. I'll just have to live vicariously through you and Lee."

"You're going to be disappointed."

"You've decided?"

"Yes. Well, maybe...yes."

"Ah," Peter said, his tone way too superior for a guy who'd been dumped by a ski bunny. "The man with the iron will speaks."

"This isn't an easy decision."

"Sure it is. You love her. She loves you. What's the problem?"

"You know it's not that simple, Peter."

"Yeah, okay. I guess. So you guys coming to lunch?"

"Of course."

"Cool. We'll talk about it there."

"No! We will not talk about it. There or anywhere else." There was a long pause. Trevor heard the shower shut off.

"Did anyone ever tell you you don't share well with others?" Peter said, finally.

"Yes."

Another dramatic sigh wafted over the airwaves. "I'll see you later."

"Bye." Trevor hung up the phone. He tried to breathe calmly, but that wasn't easy when he thought he might be having a heart attack. She was going to open that door any second. The question was, how? Dressed? In a towel? Naked as Miss July?

He took a step toward the kitchen. The coffee. That was done. He'd just get a cup. Then he stopped. He didn't want coffee. He turned toward the hallway. He needed a towel. For his shower. His cold shower.

No, maybe coffee first. He turned again and headed toward the kitchen.

"Is that a new dance? Is it anything like the Lambada?"

Trevor froze. He hadn't heard her open the door. She didn't sound naked. He turned his head slowly. When he saw that she was dressed, he relaxed. But he couldn't deny that he was disappointed.

"What?"

"Nothing. Coffee's ready."

"Good."

"The paper is, too."

"Also good. Thanks. Are you okay?"

"Yeah. Sure. Fine. Never better."

She frowned. "This is about sex, isn't it?"

He nodded.

She walked toward him, her long hair sleek and wet, her skin so clean and luminous he wanted to touch it with both hands. "Maybe it wasn't such a good idea," she said.

"What?"

"Sex."

"Oh, yeah." He forced himself to look at something that didn't turn him on. The radiator.

"You want to just forget it?" she asked, although he could hear she wasn't sure.

"Maybe that's not such a bad idea."

"I know. It was kind of nuts. I mean, we have something really special here. I'd hate to ruin that."

"Yeah, that was my concern. You're too important to me. I don't like the idea of risking that."

"I know," she said, smiling a little. "Let's just skip it. It was a crazy idea. Forget it."

He looked at Lee. She'd pushed her hair back. Curled the sides behind her ears. One tiny wisp of hair hadn't made it, though. He reached out to help, and his fingertips brushed her cheek. That was all. That was enough.

He leaned down to kiss her.

3

HE WAS going to kiss her, she realized. No, wait. He wasn't.

Trevor's head jerked back and he turned sharply to the left, almost bumping into the wall before making his way into the kitchen.

He busied himself with the coffee, avoiding her glance, but not quite able to hide the flush on his cheeks. He *had* wanted to kiss her, but he'd balked, changed his mind midlunge.

She needed to think about this. Without waiting for her coffee, she went to the big burgundy couch that dominated the living room and settled into the right corner. She pulled her sections of the paper close, then spread out the sports page. But she didn't read it. She just stared, letting the words blur.

Trevor had intended to kiss her, even if the urge had only lasted for a second. And that was *after* she'd said they should forget about sex. After he'd agreed. Obviously, he was entertaining the same kind of doubts she was. To do it? Or not to do it? That was, indeed, the question.

"You, uh, want a muffin or something?" Trevor asked, still behind the safety of the half wall that separated the living room from the kitchen.

"What do you have?" she asked, not ready to look at him yet. She didn't want him to know how confused she was, and Trevor could read her like a memo.

"Frosted Flakes," he said.

"That's not a muffin."

"I know. I don't have any muffins."

She laughed. "I'll pass."

"Okay," he said. "I'm out of milk, anyway."

Lee shook her head. He really was quite high up on her adorable scale, which was one of the reasons she felt that sleeping with him would be terrific. She just knew he'd be funny. Well, not every minute, but when it was appropriate, he'd make her laugh. There were few things she liked better than laughing in bed. For some reason, it always made her incredibly horny, at least when there was a naked man next to her. Laughing at David Letterman seldom did the trick.

"Here," he said.

She jumped, shaking the papers on her lap. She hadn't heard him come into the room. He stood next to her, holding out her coffee mug. The one that said, I Bitch, Therefore I Am. He'd bought it for her. Sentimental fool.

"I'm going to shower," he said, as she took the cup from his outstretched hand.

"Trevor, can I ask you a question?"

"No."

She waited for him to smile, but he didn't.

"You don't even know what the question is."

"If it's not about the Yankees, the weather, or work, I don't want to hear it."

"Okay, okay," she said, sinking back on the couch, marveling that Trevor was so unbalanced. She'd seen him with all sorts of women—from waitresses to district judges—on the double dates Katy was always setting them up with, but she'd never seen him lose his equilibrium.

She let him go, glad now that she hadn't asked him if he'd thought about kissing her. His whole attitude was his answer.

Her answer, despite the lapse in the shower, was still the same. If they could get past this awkward phase, she was convinced they could have something fabulous together. She rarely had powerful intuitions. But when she did, they always turned out to be right on the money.

It might take some time for this thing to happen, but what difference did that make? She had time and he wasn't going anywhere. Actually, going slowly made a great deal of sense. They had a lot on the line, and she didn't want to risk doing anything hasty.

Okay. She was going to do this thing. They were going to do it together. What had been a hazy question this morning was now a solid decision. It felt right. It felt good.

It felt scary as hell.

TREVOR TOOK HIS SEAT at the round table in the busy café. It was always the same—Lee, him, Katy, Ben, Susan and Peter. All in a nice circle of boy-girl-boy-girl. The only time it changed was when someone, usually Peter, brought a guest. But in the four years they'd been coming to the Broadway Diner, that hadn't happened more than six times.

Their Sunday brunch had become a sacred ritual. The waiters knew them so well that only minutes after the first person arrived, the lox, bagels, cream cheese and all the accoutrements were on the table. Coffee and juice poured. Even Peter's dill pickle for later was boxed and ready.

Trevor liked it this way. He was a man comfortable with rituals and routines. He woke every day at the same time. He went to sleep every night after Charlie Rose on PBS. He read the paper the same way every morning, answered his E-mail, checked his stocks, then shifted into work mode.

He picked up his napkin and placed it on his lap just as Susan and Peter walked up to the table. Ben and Katy were already there. The waiter filled his coffee cup, and Trevor relaxed for the first time this morning. He felt safe again. Among friends. Knee-deep in the familiar. All that business of sleeping with Lee was now on hold, at least for the next hour and a half.

"So," Susan said, grabbing a poppy seed bagel from the platter on the table, "did you two hit the sheets yet?"

So much for safety.

"No, we didn't." Lee sent a stern look around the table. "And you guys have to quit asking. This isn't going to happen overnight."

"I thought it wasn't going to happen at all." Yet somehow Trevor wasn't surprised that Lee had changed her mind again.

"Oh, that," Lee said, waving a dismissive hand in the air. "Ignore that. I just went spooky for a minute, that's all."

"I'm still spooky."

"No one needs to be spooky at all," Katy said. "The whole matter of you two sleeping together can be settled quickly and sanely."

Ben frowned at his wife. People often mistook them for brother and sister, they looked so much alike. Dark hair, slender, around the same height. Katy was convinced they had been related in many lifetimes. But then, that was Katy. "Honey," Ben said. "I don't think they should risk something as important as their friendship based on some pop psychology quiz."

"Pop psychology quiz? Did I say anything about a pop psychology quiz?"

Ben shook his head. "Okay, so what's your quick and sane method?"

Katy picked up half an egg bagel and started spreading it with cream cheese. "Nothing," she said.

Ben sighed. He reached over and stilled her hand with his own. "Come on, Katy. I'm sorry. I didn't mean anything. If you have a solution, we'd like to hear it."

"I wouldn't," Trevor said, even though he knew everyone was going to ignore him.

"I think Lee's right," Peter said. "It makes a lot of

sense for you two to get together. It's a jungle out
there. Dangerous. Filled with wicked people who'd
like nothing better than to get a person all hot and
bothered about them, only to wake up one morning
and announce they're going back to Idaho to fulfill a
lifelong dream of becoming a ski instructor."

Susan shook her head. "Bobby?"

Peter nodded.

"I won't say I told you so," she said, patting Peter
on the shoulder. "But dammit, I told you so."

"Susan, you wouldn't like him if he were the
Pope," Peter said with a sigh. "Someone pass the
lox."

"If he were the Pope, he wouldn't be dating you,
now would he?" Susan said. "But you're right. No
offense, but if you're going to get yourself involved
with men, you're going to pay the price. It's just the
way things are."

"Thanks," Ben said.

"Present company excepted," she said brightly.

Trevor felt bad for the guy. Peter was a wonderful
actor and a hell of a guy, but he had terrible taste in
men. He always seemed to pick the ones who were
emotionally unavailable.

That's why he and Susan got along so well. Her ex-
husband Larry was the all-time award-winning SOB.
He'd taken her for her money, slept with her sister,
and dumped her for his secretary. Susan had han-
dled it quite well. She'd decided to swear off all men
for all time, and plotted revenge for a hobby. She
seemed to delight in tormenting the men that pur-

sued her, and there were plenty of those. Susan was the only blond in the bunch. Tall, slender, Nordic-looking with pale-blue eyes, she attracted men like a magnet. But she would have none of them. They were all potential Larrys to her.

"I think you two need to just get it over with," Susan said, looking seriously at Trevor. "The longer you delay it, the more time you'll have to screw things up. I mean, come on. Think of all those wretched double dates Katy's always forcing you two into. You always end up spending the evening entertaining each other while your poor dates wither on the sidelines."

Ben draped an arm around Katy. "I think they shouldn't do anything too fast. It's a big deal. Not to be taken lightly."

"*I* think we should all just eat our damn bagels and talk about something else," Trevor said. He took a bialy and prepared it with a vengeance. Extra cream cheese. Four tomato slices. A pile of lox.

"I still want to hear what Katy has to say." Lee stirred her coffee the way she always did when she was nervous.

Trevor wanted to tell her to eat. She'd barely nibbled on her breakfast, which wasn't good for her. Worrying about Lee had become as much a ritual as brushing his teeth. Not that she ever listened to his advice. But he kept giving it to her anyway.

Of course, she did the same to him. God, they were already a couple. They just lived in separate apartments, and, well, there was the sex thing.

That sex thing was a doozy. It was tempting as hell. She was so perfect, and he already loved her so much. But maybe the reason he loved her was because she didn't ask anything of him, except friendship. She didn't get upset when he had to change plans. She didn't need to know where he was every minute of his day. She didn't even mind when he made fun of her odd penchant for *The Simpsons*.

It was very good, what they had. The best thing in his life.

"First," Katy said, wiping a stray dab of cream cheese from the corner of her mouth. "You need to ask yourself three questions. What do I really want? Will getting closer enhance the relationship, or put too big a strain on it?" Katy cleared her throat, and as if anticipating the weight of her words, the restaurant noise dimmed to a soft murmur. Trevor felt himself tense, although he wasn't sure why.

"And here's the big one. What happens if one of you or both of you fall in love?"

"With each other?" Lee blurted out.

"Yes." Katy nodded. "You have to consider it. You're moving into emotional territory. Barriers are going to break down. Intimacy is a strong and powerful thing. It can change things in a heartbeat."

Trevor looked at Lee. She looked back, blinking, as if the concept of falling in love with him was so foreign it had never once occurred to her.

It had occurred to him. That was the trouble. It had occurred to him plenty.

He had no misconceptions about his shortcomings. He couldn't dance. He was allergic to strawberries. And he couldn't commit to a relationship. Couldn't, wouldn't. It didn't matter as the outcome was the same. If Lee fell in love with him, there was no way he wouldn't hurt her. And if he fell...well, he wouldn't. That's all. Just thinking about it, a fist of panic squeezed his chest.

"Don't worry," Lee said softly. "I love you too much to fall in love with you. I wouldn't do that to my worst enemy, let alone my best friend."

THAT EVENING, Lee poured some dry food in the cat bowls, which sparked George and Ira into a frenzy of leg rubbing and loud conversation. She petted them both which was their signal to eat.

She watched them for a while. George was bigger than his brother, but Ira was a real fireball. He held his own against the orange tabby, often committing unprovoked paw batting when poor George was sound asleep. George, on the other hand, was content to sit on the window box all day without so much as a by-your-leave to her or Ira.

Next life, she was coming back as a cat.

In this life, she still had to get ready for the week ahead. Plan her meals, get her clothes together, go to the market. Figure out what the hell she was going to do about Trevor.

She went to her desk and got out her date book. Oh, God. She and Trevor were supposed to go out on a double date next week. She'd have to think about that. Maybe they shouldn't. On the other hand, maybe it would be the best thing. She was too tired to think about that now.

Then there was lunch on Tuesday with Katy, right after Katy's appointment with the doctor. She hoped that, please, *please,* this time would mean good news. Katy and Ben deserved a break. Their struggle to get pregnant had gone from the sublime to the ridiculous. Lee remembered when they'd first decided to go for it. How they'd been like kids in the candy store, having sex at every opportunity, as excited as they'd been when they were newlyweds. But nothing happened. He'd been checked, she'd been checked. Nothing was wrong. They were both able to have kids. Unfortunately, Katy's eggs hadn't gotten the message.

This new doctor might be just the ticket. Lee sure hoped so. Ben and Katy were the best couple she'd ever known. They deserved kids, and kids deserved them.

If only she'd been able to find someone like Ben. Or been as adept at relationships as Katy. It didn't do any good to lament the woeful truth, and she'd told herself a hundred times to stop wishing for things that could never be, but she couldn't help it. It was a wound that wouldn't heal, and even though it hurt, she continued to prod and poke, to rehash her mistakes until she just couldn't face them anymore.

She had tried. Lord knows, she had. Three relationships, all of them filled with hope and promise in the beginning, each one of them ending in dismal failure.

Josh, from college. Bright, funny, painfully handsome. She'd never guessed he could be cruel enough to invite her to his wedding exactly three weeks after he'd dumped her, claiming he wasn't ready for marriage.

Adam, the man she was sure would be her husband. Witty, talented, an extraordinary lover. He'd gambled away every penny she'd saved. He'd married a keno girl in Atlantic City, but at least he'd had the decency to wait a whole month.

And then there was Carl. The man she'd loved in a way that changed everything. She'd never experienced anything so powerful before or since. Three years, they'd lived in his Chelsea loft. He'd been her mentor, her friend, her lover. His success as a broker had been meteoric, but he'd kept a level head and a wicked sense of humor. It had all been perfect, right up to the day he'd left her the note giving her two days to move out so he could be free to marry a woman he'd known a week.

She'd cried until there were no more tears. Wrote pages and pages in her journal, pouring her heart out on paper. Her friends, especially Trevor, had given her the strength to go on.

It was Carl who finally helped her see that she was never going to have what Ben and Katy had. That no man was ever going to love her the way Ben loved Katy.

Not one of those men had been in love with her. They'd never even pretended, or said the word in bed. She'd loved them, even though she'd known they didn't love her back.

Never again.

If Trevor decided he didn't want to change their relationship, she'd be fine. She'd adjust. Maybe, in time, she'd meet someone else she could trust enough to sleep with. Someone she was absolutely sure she would never love.

It wasn't so horrible. She had so many blessings— her career, her friends, her cats. Even though she'd lost her mother so young, she had people to turn to for advice and comfort. She'd never really been lonely, or afraid to spend time alone. True, it was kind of sad. Sad that she'd have to miss out on that very big part of life. But then, it wasn't a tragedy, either. It didn't even preclude her having children. She could always adopt, or have artificial insemination. No, she'd be fine. She'd be great.

But she sure would like it if she and Trevor could take that one last step. Because the truth was, she missed being held. She missed it so much, it made her ache inside.

She could just picture the two of them, lying in her big bed underneath the white comforter. Watching some great old movie, sharing popcorn and root beer. Touching. Laughing. Holding each other through the long nights.

No commitments, no promises, no broken hearts. Just kindness and affection and a sweetness that only Trevor was capable of.

Ira jumped up on her desk, and sat down right on

top of her date book. He looked at her with his inquisitive green eyes, and even before she touched him, she could hear his rumbling purr.

As she rubbed his ears, she smiled. Maybe she didn't need to wait until her next life to be as contented as a cat. If things went well, which she just knew they would, she and Trevor could both be snug in the knowledge that they were safe. That their needs were being met. That they wouldn't hurt each other or leave each other. It would be perfect.

All they had to do was get past this awkward phase.

4

TREVOR KNEW it was Lee before he picked up the phone. No way she was going to chalk up tonight's fiasco of a double date without rehashing every detail. He'd grown used to her blow-by-blow analyses, and most of the time he didn't mind them. Lee's wit and sharp tongue made her monologues as interesting as a Fran Lebowitz column, and with Lee, Trevor knew all the players.

Except tonight he was one of the players, and he wasn't terribly keen on discussing the minutiae of his blunders until one in the morning.

He lifted the receiver.

"Did you kiss Connie good-night?" Lee asked.

"Well, hi to you, too. No, I didn't. What about you?"

"He kissed my cheek."

"Which one?"

She paused. "The one on my face."

"Ah," he said, walking to the fridge. Inside he found several bottles of Corona, milk, orange juice and Bloody Mary mix, in addition to a couple of nice bottles of a California chardonnay he'd recently reviewed for the magazine. Four stars. But it was late, so the orange juice won. He grabbed the plastic carton and shut the fridge door with his foot, then walked over to his big velvet chair and let himself sink into the familiar contours.

"What I can't understand is how Katy could have ever imagined I'd like him," Lee said. "Could the man talk about anything but breasts? I mean, please. Like I care about the advantages of saline over silicone?"

"He did offer to give you a good discount."

"I don't need bigger boobs," she said, and he heard the sound of meowing cats in the background. She must be feeding the boys. "Do I?"

"No, you don't," he said, picturing her breasts, then instantly breaking out in a cold sweat.

"Are you sure? You haven't really seen them, you know."

"I can tell they're just great, Lee." He wiped the perspiration off his forehead and wished she'd change the subject. But at least if he passed out from unrequited lust, she'd call the paramedics for him. "You don't need bigger anything."

"Okay. Here sweeties. Salmon, yummy!"

"Lee?"

"What?"

"If you're going to make yummy noises for your cats, I'm leaving."

"Keep your shirt on. I just have to change their water."

Trevor took the opportunity to open the orange juice carton and take a healthy swig. The sweet drink helped dissipate the sour taste left over from to-night's disaster.

Katy had convinced them to go through with it, insisting that it was the perfect time to see other people. Then they would be able to take a more well-rounded look at what he'd come to think of as "The Plan." So, tonight he had gone out with a lawyer from Ben's office and Lee had gone out with a plastic surgeon friend of Katy's. They'd gone to a concert at Lincoln Center and then for Chinese after. It should have been nice. They'd done the same thing before, with different dates, of course, and they'd always had a decent time.

Not tonight.

For the first time since college, he'd been uncomfortable around one of Lee's dates. The breast discussions hadn't helped. Greg, the doctor, hadn't been able to go five minutes without mentioning nipples, for God's sake. Was it any wonder Trevor couldn't stop thinking about Lee's breasts? That he'd had to fight the urge to touch her all through Rhapsody in Blue?

"You there?"

"Yep."

"Trevor?"

"Hmm?"

"Tonight showed me everything I need to know. Dammit, let's stop wasting all this time and energy on people we don't like. I say we get off our tushies and get down to some serious boinking."

Trevor jerked as a small jet of orange juice shot out

of the top of the carton. He hadn't realized he'd been squeezing it so hard. He took another drink, wishing he'd added vodka.

"Well?"

Despite the bravado of her words, there was a hint of nervousness in her voice. Maybe not. Maybe he was the only one scared out of his mind. Either way, he wasn't going to rush this. It was too important. He thought about Connie, his date. She'd been very pretty and smart. Funny, too. Just the kind of woman he liked. Used to like. Tonight, she just wasn't Lee. And that was that.

So what was he so worried about? He wanted to be with Lee. She wanted to be with him. They both understood the formula—sex plus friendship minus complications.

Sex with Lee. Good God, the thought had taken permanent residence in his brain, right where good sense used to live. Now that it was there, it wasn't going to go away. Not until he did something about it.

He took in a big breath of air, and let it out slowly, preparing for the dive off the high board. "Okay," he said, knowing that one little word was going to open a completely new chapter of his life. That things would never be the same again. It might be wonderful, just like Lee predicted. Or he might be signing the death warrant to the best friendship he'd ever had.

"Wow."

"Yeah, wow. Dammit, Lee, what if—"

"Stop. Stop right there. We can't do what if. We have to believe it's going to be perfect."

"That's easy for you, Pollyanna, but for those of us in the real world, the future holds some risks."

"What doesn't? Hell, you could be hit by a taxi tomorrow morning."

"Impeccable logic. Nonsense, but impeccable."

"It's not nonsense. I simply choose to have an optimistic point of view, which, sweet cheeks, is one of the things you like most about me."

"I think you're confusing optimism with fatalism."

"Oh, my God."

"What?"

"I just realized something. Having sex means we're going to be naked. With each other. I mean, I have really good boobs for a platonic relationship, but now that we're upgrading to platonic gold—"

"Platonic gold?"

"Yeah, like Visa gold. You still have the same card, but you get more perks."

Trevor grinned. "Perks, huh? Beats the hell out of a free rental car."

"I'm serious," she said. "We're talking about actually getting naked. In front of each other."

"I already know what you look like," he said. That's all he'd been thinking about for days, but he wasn't about to tell her that.

"You do not."

"I've seen you in a bathing suit."

"It's not the same."

"Is there something you need to tell me? This isn't going to turn out like *The Crying Game,* is it?"

She laughed. "No. All I'm saying is, you haven't seen all the parts yet."

"Uh-huh."

"And I haven't seen all your parts."

He inhaled sharply, feeling his parts stir.

"Other *mysterious* parts," Lee whispered.

Her tone had changed. The humor was now laced with something more. Something daring and intimate. She wasn't kidding anymore.

Trevor shifted on his chair, wondering if he should hang up the phone. Or maybe rip it out of the wall. This was it. The moment of change. He could still back out. There was still time. "I don't have anything you haven't seen before."

"I haven't seen *you.* And now..."

"What?"

"I need to see it."

A surge of lust hit him so hard, he nearly fell on the floor. He struggled to regain his composure. To keep things light. "I can hold it up to the phone, if you think it'll help."

"I'm not kidding. I need to see you naked, Trevor."

"If..." The word came out an octave too high. He cleared his throat and started again. "When we do it, you'll see it all."

"No," she said. "I need to see it first."

"What are you talking about?"

"I have to see it. You. Before we move to the next step."

"Why?" He closed his eyes, wondering what he'd done to deserve this torture.

"Because. I just need to, okay?"

A horrible thought struck him. "What is this, some kind of test? Are you going to change your mind if it's not big enough?"

"No! No, that's not it at all."

He waited for her explanation, but it wasn't forthcoming. All he could hear was her rapid breathing. All he could think about were parts, his and hers, and how crazy this all was. Crazy that he was even thinking about seeing her naked. About touching her, tasting her. Holding her in his arms.

He closed his eyes and pictured her in front of him. It was so easy. He knew her so well. The way the light made her hair shine like fire. The crooked front tooth that she constantly complained about that actually made her look even prettier. Her legs. Oh, God. He couldn't go there. Not to her legs. This wasn't good. He shouldn't be thinking these thoughts. They were far too dangerous. He'd never allowed himself to want her, because he knew he couldn't have her.

Now, it seemed the floodgates had opened. Ever since she'd first brought up the idea of sleeping together, he'd thought of little else. The need must have been there for a long time. Just under the surface. He woke up with Lee on his mind. And fell asleep the same way. Whether he liked it or not, he'd crossed the line. He doubted seriously he'd ever be able to go back.

"I need to take this in order," Lee said, finally. "Small steps. I want to get over the naked thing first. It's going to be awkward, we both know that. But if we do it in a nonthreatening way, we can get over the awkwardness. Then, we can move on to the next step."

"And these two steps can't take place at the same time?"

"No. I know you think I'm nuts, but indulge me, please."

"How is this supposed to work?"

"You'll come over. No, maybe not here. And not at your place. We'll figure out where. And then—"

"We get naked."

"No. *You* get naked."

The lush image in his mind vanished with a poof. "What? Are you kidding?"

"I'm the one that needs this step. You don't."

"I'm not going to get naked by myself."

"Why not?"

"Because it's ridiculous, that's why."

"It's not. It's just the way it needs to be."

"Lee, I'll get naked all you want. But only if there's quid pro quo."

She giggled. It was such a great sound. Not a girlie giggle, nothing like that. Lee giggled low, a throaty, sexy kind of half laugh. "Can you believe this? We're actually gonna do it."

"Yeah," he said. He put the orange juice carton on

the coffee table, then leaned back in the chair. He was still a little hard. With just a bit of concentration he could be a lot hard. Uh-oh. "I need to go," he said.

"We're not finished."

"Yes, we are."

"But—"

"Good night, Lee. We'll talk in the morning."

"Come for lunch."

"Okay. Now good night."

"Trevor?"

"What?"

"I have auburn hair."

"*What?*"

She giggled again. "Think about it. Nighty night."

He stared at the phone after she hung up. And then it hit him. She had *auburn hair.* Oh, dammit.

LEE OPENED her desk drawer to look for a pack of gum, but all she could come up with was an eraser, a fuzzy breath mint, and two ticket stubs to a play at the Manhattan Theater Club. She closed the drawer, then tried to signal Eleanor, the broker who sat at the next desk, but Eleanor had a phone at each ear and wasn't paying any attention to Lee. She debated throwing the eraser at her colleague, but changed her mind and focused in on her own phone conversation again.

Mr. Wilkins had been talking for ten minutes. Lee had clocked it. No breaks, hardly any breaths, and he hadn't mentioned his portfolio once. However, she did know about his tomatoes, the noisy neighbors downstairs and the man at the corner market who wore women's clothes. She really had better things to do. Phone calls, fact checking, getting some more coffee. But she wouldn't be brusque with Mr. Wilkins. He was so lonely since his wife died that Lee didn't have the heart to hurry him up. Besides, Trevor was due any minute, so she'd make her calls after lunch.

"No, Mr. Wilkins, I haven't seen that episode of *Murder, She Died.*"

"It's a good one, let me tell you. That Angela Lindbergh, she's the best actress in the country."

"I like her, too," Lee said, smiling. Mr. Wilkins had a propensity for mixing up words which was pretty amusing. She reached over and tapped on her mouse pad, waking up her computer. A spreadsheet instantly replaced her *Far Side* screen saver.

"Anyway," he said, drawing out the word until it was just a sigh.

Lee relaxed. He'd gotten tired, that word was her clue. They only had a minute of business to take care of. "So what do you think about rolling over that money in the mutual fund?"

"Whatever you think is right, Lee."

"It's your money, not mine."

"I know. But you've taken good care of me for two years. I trust you."

"Thanks for the vote of confidence. I think it's a pretty safe investment, and it's holding steady. So I'll go ahead and roll it over, if you're sure."

"I am. I couldn't be in better hands."

Lee smiled, but not just in response to Mr. Wilkins's kind words. Trevor had arrived. As he walked down the corridor, she watched her fellow brokers check him out. They'd all seen him before, but Trevor wasn't someone they could ignore. All the women and three-quarters of the men would like to roll him over if they had the chance.

She said goodbye to Mr. Wilkins and hung up the phone just as Trevor got to her desk. "Howdy," she said, urging the butterflies in her stomach to take a hike. Last night's conversation was still fresh in her mind. Too fresh. She felt a hot blush fill her cheeks, and there wasn't a thing she could do about it.

"Howdy, yourself," he said.

He looked damn good. He'd worn her favorite black slacks, the ones that hugged his long legs and made his butt look fabulous. And the gray silk shirt she'd given him last Christmas. Altogether a delicious combination. He'd pushed back his hair with his fingers, which mussed it up just right.

It was odd and scary to think about him like this. She'd watched other women drool over Trevor for years, but she'd never indulged. Given her enthusiasm now, it seemed clear that she'd been suppressing her feelings for a long time.

"You look nice," he said, his slow grin making his face even more handsome.

"Thanks." She had taken special care today. She'd gotten up early to wash and set her hair, and she'd picked the black Donna Karan that she usually reserved for important business dinners.

"Where are we going?"

She got her purse from the bottom drawer of her desk and stood up. "How about that Thai place?"

"Sounds good," he said, as his gaze darted down. Right to her breasts. Then up again to her face.

"Although we could just go to my apartment," she said, careful to keep her voice down so that all the busybodies she worked with wouldn't hear. They already speculated about her relationship with Trevor, and were highly suspect of her sex life in general. Not once in the three years she'd worked at the brokerage had she accepted an invitation from one of her male co-workers. Business, yes. Personal, never. So they either thought she was lying about just being friends with Trevor, or they thought she was gay. Neither bothered her. She liked to keep her private life private. But if he kept looking at her like that, she might jump his bones right here. "Well?" she prodded.

"I don't think so," Trevor said. "Going to your place seems pretty dangerous."

"Suit yourself." She led him down the path between the cubicles, calling over her shoulder, "Chicken."

"You got that right."

He caught up with her at the elevator. A crowd mingled, as most people on this floor, hell, in the whole building, went to lunch at noon. She'd had to wait for fifteen minutes sometimes, just to catch a ride down. She wasn't about to walk it. Not all sixty floors.

"So, have you changed your mind?" she asked, smiling up at him.

"About what?"

"What I asked you last night."

He stilled, then leaned down a bit so he could speak quietly. "Only if you've changed yours."

"Nope. It's my way or the highway."

"The highway, it is," he said just as the elevator door opened. They hustled inside, and Trevor moved all the way to the back. She stood just in front of him, hemmed in on all sides by ravenous brokers. It wasn't pretty.

"We need to talk." Trevor whispered in her right ear, so close that she felt his warm breath on her neck. An unexpected frisson raced down her back, giving her goose bumps and instant hard nipples.

She nodded, wanting him to say more. Wishing everyone else would disappear.

The elevator stopped again, and even more people clambered in. Everyone shifted a bit, then the ride continued down, stopping again on the next floor, eliciting groans from those outside when they saw there was no more room.

Packed in like sardines, the unique and uncomfortable "elevator silence" descended, which always piqued Lee's urge to say something loud and rude. She quelled it, especially after another idea popped into her head. One hell of a wild idea.

She couldn't.

He'd go nuts.

She wasn't brave enough. Not by half. Or was she?

She smiled. What the hell? He wasn't going anywhere, and neither was she. The next floor was the express, which would take them all the way down to the ground floor. The ride would last about a minute. Just enough time. Oh, God, could she get up her nerve to really do it?

Forcing herself to be slow and patient, she eased her hand back, all the way, until she found Trevor's belt. Closing her eyes, she took the plunge. She moved her hand lower, lower. There. She felt it. She had her hand right on it! Oh, God.

"What are you doing?" he whispered fiercely.

"Taking matters into my own hands," she whispered back, not moving her head at all for fear that someone would turn and catch her with her hand in the cookie jar.

"Stop it."

"Not on your life," she said, growing bolder as he grew.

"Lee!"

"Someone had to take the bull by the horns," she said, fighting the urge to laugh, "so to speak."

"You're making a big mistake."

"I don't think so. And from what I can tell, you don't mind very much. I detect some enthusiasm, unless I'm mistaken."

"You are."

She couldn't help it. She laughed, but cut it off quickly as the woman in front of her turned to look. Instead, Lee concentrated on what her hand felt. Amazed at her own audacity, she felt almost giddy.

If this didn't jump-start things between them, nothing would. And this way, she didn't even have to face him. At least not until the end of the ride, and then... Well, he'd certainly know for sure that she wasn't kidding about the sex part.

She wished his pants weren't so thick. She'd like more details. But she felt enough. My, my. That old wives' tale about shoe size was right on target.

The elevator slowed, and the door opened. Immediately, the crowd rushed out, but Lee didn't move. Her body or her hand. She wanted to wait until the last possible second to let go. God, she couldn't believe it. It was something Susan would do, not her. She just wished she could see his face.

Her wish came true.

Trevor's face appeared before her. In fact, his whole body appeared. Which wasn't possible. Because she was holding...

Trevor stepped back until he was clear of the elevator. He smiled at Lee, enjoying the way her eyes nearly popped out of her head. The lovely shade of red that started at her neck and went up to her hair.

The man behind her seemed equally flustered, which was completely understandable. Lee hadn't moved yet. The man, who Trevor guessed was in his sixties, stood stock-still. Not that he had much choice.

Trevor heard Lee say something like, "Urp." And then the elevator doors slid closed. But not before he waved goodbye to Lee and her new best friend.

5

LEE REGISTERED Trevor's jaunty wave seconds before the elevator door shut with a finality that made her yearn for a firing squad. Every muscle in her body seemed to spasm at once, and a sharp "Ouch" from behind her reminded her that she hadn't let go. She opened her hand and leapt to the other side of the elevator, feeling her stomach drop as the elevator soared upward.

All she wanted to do was run and hide, or better yet, put a hole through the floor of the cab and plunge to a grateful death. Instead, she forced herself to look at the man she'd groped.

He was older, maybe in his sixties, with thick white hair, glasses and even teeth. His cheeks looked flushed, but other than that, he seemed remarkably composed, given the circumstances.

"I...I..."

"You know," the man said calmly, "in all the years I've taken this elevator, I never met anyone. For what it's worth, your introduction was top-notch."

Lee knew her blush could cook eggs. And when she let her gaze drop to the man's pants, she felt as if she were going to burst into flames. "I...I'm so sorry," she said. "It was a mistake."

The man laughed. "One hell of a doozy, I'd say."

"You were supposed to be someone else."

"Well, then, I guess this is my lucky day."

She blinked several times, trying to make some sense of her panicked thoughts. "You're not going to call the police?"

He shook his head. "Why, were you trying to rob me?"

She shook her head.

"Good," he said. "Because if you were, you'd need a lot of practice."

Just then the elevator came to a stop. The doors opened with a little whoosh, and even though she wanted to run as fast as she could, her feet didn't move. Nothing moved but her heart, which pounded so hard she felt sure a coronary was seconds away. The white-haired man walked past her, and as people filed in, he reached into his pocket, drew out a card, and handed it to her. "Just in case," he said.

Then, mercifully, he stepped out and the doors closed. Two floors up, Lee finally looked at the card. "John Farmer, Esq., Attorney at Law." She closed her eyes and sighed. At least when she killed Trevor, she'd have a sympathetic lawyer.

TREVOR SAW HER as she stepped out of the elevator. She spotted him a second later and he realized, too late, that he should have made a run for it when he'd had the chance. If looks could kill, he'd be a dead man.

She walked toward him, her purse swinging dangerously in her right hand, her gaze burning a hole in his forehead. He backed up, hitting the side of the newsstand. "I tried to warn you," he said.

"Don't." The single word was a warning, one a smart man would have heeded.

"I told you you were making a mistake."

Lee opened her mouth, then closed it again, opting instead to slug him in the shoulder. Hard.

"Ouch."

"Ouch, my ass. I could kill you for this."

"Hey, don't blame me. I wasn't the one who wanted to play grope-in-the-elevator."

"I've never been so humiliated in my life. Dammit, Trevor, why did you let me—" She slugged him again. In the same spot.

He moved, offering his other shoulder, and she gave him another good one. "Are you finished?"

"No. I'm going to hit you every chance I get. You deserve worse, you snake. You could have stopped me."

He grinned. "But that wouldn't have been any fun."

Lee crossed her arms, and he said a silent thanks. His shoulders couldn't take much more.

"I can't believe you. Of all the low, underhanded, dirty, rotten—"

"How did this become my fault? You were hoisted, my dear, on your own petard."

"I'll show you a petard," she said, uncrossing her arms.

Trevor started moving backward, clearing the newsstand so he could head toward the front door. He didn't take his eyes off Lee, though. "Now come on. You have to admit, it was funny."

"Funny? *Funny?* I felt up a complete stranger in public. You find that amusing?"

"Well, yeah."

Her arms went up and out, the purse swinging wildly from the end of her hand. He ducked, but the display of Tic Tacs right behind him had no defensive maneuvers at all. They went flying, little bullets of fresh breath hitting people in dark suits. Lee didn't care. She was on the rampage, and woe to the person who got in her way.

"I'm kidding," he said, holding up his hand in a gesture of acquiescence. "I didn't say anything because I didn't know how to do it without embarrassing you."

"Oh, good. That was considerate. Leaving me with some strange, aroused man in a tiny enclosed space was much better."

"Honey, the way you had him, he wasn't about to do anything to make you angry."

"That isn't the point. You should have stopped me."

He could see she was losing steam. Thank God. The employees at the Wall Street high-rise had given them a wide berth, and he had the feeling the gendarmes would be coming soon. Knowing instinctively that Lee wouldn't like jail, he started picking up Tic Tac containers. Lee helped by burying her face in her hands.

By the time the slightly wounded display was back together, and Trevor had given the newsstand guy ten bucks for his trouble, Lee seemed composed again. Angry, but composed.

"You okay?" he asked.

She nodded, still giving him the evil eye. "I won't forgive you for this. Ever."

"Sure you will."

She sighed. "I know. But you can't tell anyone."

He suppressed a laugh. If she thought he was going to keep this one to himself, she had another think coming.

"Trevor?"

The way she said his name told him she was thinking about hitting him again, so he nodded. "Okay, okay."

"Promise?"

"I won't tell anyone except Susan."

"If you tell Susan, greater Manhattan will know by sundown."

He got brave and put his arm around Lee's shoulder. It was meant to be a comfort, a friendly gesture to avoid making a promise he knew damn well he couldn't keep. But the second he touched her and felt her warm, soft shoulder, he was instantly aware of her body. His body. All those parts.

He let go with a jerk.

"What's wrong?"

"Nothing," he said, increasing the distance between them.

"That is not a nothing's-wrong face."

He looked around at all the people who had gathered around them. This was a whole new group who hadn't been here for the flying Tic Tacs. No one was paying them any mind, and he didn't want to get their attention.

"Well?" Lee looked at him quizzically, her right hand on her right hip. Her little black dress curved and dipped making him achingly aware of what lay beneath the material. He suddenly had the urge to ask her into an elevator.

"Hello?" she prompted.

He snapped his attention back to Lee's face. "Lunch," he said. "I'm starving."

She shook her head, then shrugged. Trevor made absolutely sure they didn't touch as they left the building, or as they walked down Pearl Street. But his gaze kept sliding over, watching her hair glitter in the sunlight, the way she walked with easy confidence and grace. Next time Lee had the urge to grope someone, he was going to make sure he was squarely in the line of fire.

A LITTLE GIRL, maybe three or four, stood up on tiptoe trying to slip the envelope in the corner mailbox. Her father, at least Lee assumed he was her father, stood very close behind her, urging her on, his hands poised to lift her if she couldn't make the stretch. She finally did make it, and let the letter go, squealing with delight at her monumental accomplishment. Her father scooped her up in his arms, hugged her close and the two of them giggled as they waded through the after-work crowd on Fifth Avenue.

Lee watched them until the crush of people in front of FAO Schwartz swallowed them up. She sighed, the ache that had become as much a part of her as her breath squeezed her chest and sent her mood spiraling down.

Lee had decided a while ago that a lifelong relationship was not for her. But she couldn't deny the truth. She wanted her own little girl. She wanted her own husband. It didn't seem as if it were too much to ask, but evidently it was. Katy insisted that twenty-seven was too young to give up the fight, but Katy didn't understand. How could she, when she had Ben next to her? Lee was just plain tired of beating her head against the wall. Of facing failure over and over, of trying to move on, and act as if her heart wasn't permanently damaged. Something was wrong with her. Some missing gene, or a mental quirk, or bad karma, or who the hell knew what, except that it always ended the same way. Her falling in love, him not loving her back. Him getting married weeks later to someone who wasn't damaged. Three times.

She might not be a Nobel laureate, but even she could see the pattern. Love wasn't in the stars for her. It just wasn't her destiny. She'd accepted her fate, and made peace with it. Except for sometimes. Except for when she saw little girls on tiptoe. When she heard a giggle float down Fifth Avenue. Then the unfairness of it all threatened to burst inside her, filling every crevice in her soul with shrapnel.

It took all her strength to turn away from the mailbox and the image of the little girl that still lingered in her mind's eye. She breathed deeply, willing herself to snap out of it. To smile. To focus on all she did have, instead of what wasn't to be hers.

Trevor. She had Trevor. That was a hell of a lot. He loved her the best way he knew how. While it wasn't the kind of love that she longed for, it was enough. It had to be.

She just wished they could get on with it. If she could sleep with him, if she could feel his body next to hers, then the ache would go away. She was sure of it. With Trevor, there would be no false hope. No dreaming about a wedding, or a baby. He would give her comfort, and she would give it right back.

Of course, first they'd have to get over this little problem of being naked. But she'd thought a lot about that this afternoon. After the debacle in the elevator, she wasn't going to press Trevor into dropping his trousers for her. That was too dangerous. Instead, she'd decided that they'd have to undress under the covers. At night. With the lights out.

Later on, she wouldn't care, but she knew enough about herself to know that the first time was going to be a little awkward. The more she thought about it beforehand, the more awkward the actual event was going to be. So what they needed to do was stop analyzing and start doing.

She planned to tell him that tonight, and she wasn't going to accept no for an answer.

"What are you smiling about?"

Lee whirled around to see Susan standing by the café door. She was a vision in pale-blue. A silk blouse, matching tailored slacks, and an Hermès scarf gave her an air of elegance, yet somehow also made her seem aloof. With her perfect blond hair pulled back like that, she reminded Lee of Grace Kelly. "Do you want kids?" Lee asked.

Susan's brows arched. "Right now?"

"No. Sometime."

Susan shook her head. "Nope. Having kids would mean having sex, and that would mean being with a man. So, no. I don't."

"What happened now?"

"The bastard wants my O'Keeffe. It's not enough that he wants alimony so he can stay home and work on his Great American Novel, which, by the way, is such drivel you'd get sick reading more than two pages. Now he wants my painting."

"He's not going to get it, Susan. He's just trying to rattle you."

"He's doing a fine job."

"Come on. I'll buy you a drink."

"With two cherries?"

"With six, if that will make you happy."

Susan smiled and opened the door, and Lee went into the brightly lit restaurant. It was already crowded, with a crush of business types at the bar. Everyone seemed to be drinking martinis or Manhattans. The noise level was right up there with rock concerts and jet engines, so Lee used hand signals with Ellen, the hostess. Ellen had been a neighbor when Lee lived in Queens, so finding a table for five in the back room, the quieter room, wasn't a problem.

Lee gave Ellen a five-dollar tip, and complimented her on her shoes. Ellen smiled bravely and headed back to the meat-market section of the restaurant as Lee sat down next to Susan. She waited, expecting Susan to make a comment about the elevator mishap, prepared to deny everything, but the only thing Susan said was, "Who's not coming?"

"Peter. He has to rehearse tonight." Lee signaled the waiter, and relaxed. Trevor hadn't told. She should be ashamed of herself for thinking he had.

"Be nice to Katy and Ben," Susan said. "Katy got her period."

"Oh, no." Lee sighed. Katy had been three days late, and they'd been so hopeful.

"It really stinks. Of all the people in the universe who should have children..."

The waiter, a stunning brown-haired hunk in very snug black slacks, came to the table and right to Susan. He was instantly smitten. His eyes got wide, his clean-shaven yet rugged jaw dropped. He hung on her every word, and Lee could tell that Susan would be getting her Manhattan with a whole jar of cherries on the side. When Lee ordered her white wine, the waiter barely noticed her.

Lee watched him go, then turned back to the goddess next to her. "You amaze me," she said.

"What?"

"You didn't see that? If you'd ordered an appetizer I swear he would have proposed."

Susan got that look on her face. Disgust mixed with dismissal. "They're all slime. Every one."

"They are not. You're just mad at Larry and transferring your feelings to men in general."

"Thank you, Dr. Freud. But I know what I'm talking about. The problem with you, dearest Lee, is that you insist on anthropomorphizing men. You give them all the qualities of human beings and then it breaks your heart when they don't act human."

"I do not. I happen to like men. And just because I was hurt a few times doesn't mean all men are skunks."

"You mean Trevor isn't a skunk."

"That's right. He isn't. And neither is Ben or Peter."

"Fine. Three out of six million. And speaking of Trevor, how goes the quest?"

Before she could answer, Trevor, Ben and Katy arrived at the table. Hellos were said, and Lee watched for signs that Katy was having a rough time of it, but she seemed okay. The waiter came back just then, and sure enough, he had a glassful of cherries to go with Susan's Manhattan. He took the rest of the drink orders, barely able to keep his eyes off his new inamorata, and Lee opened her menu.

Trevor sat next to her, and while she looked at the

salads, he scooted close. Closer than he needed to given the size of the table. Just as she turned her attention to the fish selections, she felt it. His hand on her thigh. Light, tentative, a little shaky, but he didn't retreat. As the seconds ticked on, her pulse shot through the roof as the pressure on her leg increased until his hand rested comfortably. The heat of his skin passed through her dress and her hose as if they weren't there. She didn't know what to do. Touch him back? Smile? Say something?

Finally, she managed to look at him. His gaze was quiet, more a question than anything else. He glanced down quickly, then she felt him squeeze her gently.

Although he touched only the top of her thigh, the sensation hit her everywhere. Her breath froze in her lungs. Her stomach clenched. She was right. As long as they stopped worrying, and they just trusted in each other, nothing was going to go wrong. They could be so much for each other. The perfect complements.

He leaned over, so he could whisper in her ear. "What are you doing this weekend?"

She shook her head, not brave enough to tell him the decision she'd made a few moments ago.

"How does a trip to Mystic sound?"

"Wonderful."

"I know a great bed-and-breakfast. Antiques, fireplaces in the bedrooms. Claw-foot tubs."

"It sounds perfect."

"Good," he said. Then he took his hand away, and turned to speak to Ben.

Lee kept looking at the menu, even though the words blurred together. The heat from where he'd touched her dissipated in a few moments. The reality of what he'd proposed took much longer to sink in.

This was it. In four days, she and Trevor were going to be more than friends. They were going to be lovers. Not like any lovers she'd ever known, and that was the beauty of it all. They were going to break the rules, explore uncharted territory. But she wasn't scared. Not too scared, at least. Because he'd be with her every step of the way.

"Lee?"

She looked up. Katy stared at her, and Lee realized she'd been trying to talk to her for a while. "Hm?"

"Split a chicken tarragon with me?"

"Sure."

"Good," Katy said, "since I intend to eat every dessert they have."

Lee closed her menu. Things were going very nicely. Trevor had obviously not told the rest of the gang about her little faux pas from this morning. She was going to have the crème brûlée for dessert. And in four days, she was going to embark on the next phase of her life. The phase without worries, without doubts.

"Oh, and listen," Katy said. "After dinner, let's all go to the Empire State Building, okay?"

Puzzled, Lee looked at Katy. "Why?"

"Because it's almost Ben's birthday. So I told him he could ride in the elevator with you."

6

"WHAT IS THAT?" Lee asked, looking at the tiny scrap of material Katy held out.

"It's underpants."

"*That's* underpants? It wouldn't cover my right toe."

"It's not supposed to." She stretched the pink garment out so it took on the vague shape of a triangular Band-Aid. "It's a thong."

"I'm not wearing a thong. Ever. I've gone all my life trying to get underwear out from where they've designed it to go in."

"You have no sense of adventure."

"I do so. I simply prefer to go on my adventures without butt floss."

Katy tossed the offending panties onto the sale table and wandered over to the teddy section of Victoria's Secret. The place was pretty crowded for seven at night on a Tuesday. Maybe it was always like this. She wouldn't know. The last time she'd gone shopping for underwear, she'd been at a Macy's sale, picking up seven pairs of identical, practical, cotton panties.

But cotton wouldn't do for this weekend. She

needed new bras, too. And something to sleep in. A robe. Basically, everything from the top down.

"This is fabulous!"

Lee turned to Susan, who held up a black silk garter belt to her waist, and frowned. "I'm not going to need a garter belt. I'm not planning on wearing stockings."

"Not for you, silly. For me. I think this would look divine with my red stilettos."

"Why do you need red stilettos when you're not dating?"

Susan waggled her brows. "I said I'm never getting involved with another man. Not that I wouldn't want a judiciously timed roll in the hay. I'm just sorry you had that idea about Trevor first. It's so brilliant, it's scary."

"Is it? I swear I'm driving myself nuts. One second I'm certain that all my problems will be solved by sleeping with Trev, and the next second I'm positive I'm ruining my life."

"Lee, the answer to that is so simple." Susan picked up a white garter belt and held it up to her waist. She admired the view in the full-length mirror, and a slim young man wearing an Elvis Costello T-shirt enjoyed it with her. Susan didn't blink. Lee supposed she'd grown so used to being ogled it didn't faze her anymore.

"I'm waiting for this great and simple revelation," Lee said, eyeing a pretty floral print matching bra and panty set.

"Quit thinking," Susan said.

"Yes. Right. That's exactly the conclusion I came to on Monday. The problem is getting my mind to concur."

"Okay, here's what you do." Susan eyed the flowered underwear in Lee's hand and gave her a disgusted look. "First, you get rid of those awful things and find yourself something sexy. Second, every time a thought about this weekend comes up, start singing 'It's A Small World.'"

"You're kidding, right? That song is evil. Once it gets into my head, it never leaves."

"Exactly."

Lee nodded. "Okay. But if I end up at Bellevue, I'm holding you personally responsible."

Susan smiled as she zeroed in on a hanging display. She pulled out a black satin set, bikini underpants and a demibra. "This is it," she said.

"I don't think so."

"I do. Now you march right in that dressing room and try this on."

"Now?"

"No. Next Christmas."

Lee took the plastic hanger and started toward the dressing room. The tag said it was a Wonder bra. She'd never tried one on before and her curiosity was piqued. There was one empty dressing room left, and she slipped inside.

She hated taking off her clothes in front of dressing room mirrors. The lighting sucked, the air felt cold and unfamiliar, and she never liked what she saw. So she rushed out of her blouse and her good old Playtex Cross Your Heart, and put on the black number. She had to adjust her breasts, lifting, separating, bending forward to make sure the fit was right, but when she looked up, she gasped.

"What's wrong?" Katy's voice came from directly outside the room.

"Holy cow. I look like Anna Nicole Smith!"

"Let me see."

Lee opened the door without taking her eyes off her new shape. The Wonder bra had lived up to its name, and more. Her breasts looked huge, which made her waist look tiny, and the black slinky material gave her skin a porcelain glow.

"Wow," Katy said.

Lee nodded.

"I gotta get me one of those."

"I'm sure Ben would like it."

"I gotta get me a whole lotta those."

Lee smiled, but as she turned to her side to look at her profile, it occurred to her that this may not be the right bra at all. "I don't know," she said. "It's kind of false advertising, isn't it?"

"You think Trevor will care?"

Lee looked up to see Susan standing right next to Katy. "He can't help but notice. Unless I never take the bra off."

"You're giving him far too much credit," Susan said. "As soon as he gets a load of you in that, all the blood will rush from his head, and he won't have the ability to give it another thought."

"You'll be lucky if he can remember your name," Katy said.

Susan nodded. "Or his own."

"Really?" Lee looked at herself full on. Surprisingly, she really liked what she saw. So what if that damn doctor had offered her a discount. This little number did the same thing, without a recovery period.

"I'll go get some more," Katy said. "What do you think? Five?"

"I'm only going to be gone for two days."

"But he'll be coming over after you get back."

"Oh, yeah."

"You don't sound very excited," Susan said. "Remember. 'It's A Small World.'"

The song started in the back of Lee's mind. She didn't know whether to hug Susan or slug her.

TREVOR LOOKED at his overnight bag, then back at the two pairs of pajamas he held in his hands. The navy blue were nicer, but they had a tear on one cuff. The gray pair were older, but in good shape. He tossed the gray pajamas on top of his toiletry kit, two shirts, slacks, socks and underwear, and looked around to see if he was missing anything. Robe? He didn't think so. Book? God, he hoped not. *Aha.*

He went to his medicine cabinet and took out his box of Trojans. He took out two, then another one. *What the hell,* he thought, and tossed the whole box into the suitcase. Better safe than sorry.

One more quick glance around the bedroom, and

then a look at his watch. Ten minutes until he had to leave to pick up Lee. He zipped up his bag, checked his wallet to make sure he had cash, then went for his jacket. It was starting to get a little chilly here in the mornings, and in Connecticut it would probably be colder.

He stepped outside, and locked his door behind him. This was it. He was really going to do it.

The anxiety was almost more than he could stand. What if...

No. He wasn't going to do that. No what ifs. No maybes. He was embarking on a mission, one that promised to change his life for the better. He could stop dreaming about being with Lee, and actually be with her. She wouldn't press him to take the relationship to the next level. She wouldn't casually take him shopping, only to wind up in housewares looking at china patterns. She wouldn't expect him to ask her to live with him, or, God forbid, propose.

With Lee, it was the best of all possible worlds. So what was he worried about?

The elevator arrived and the door opened. He stepped inside, and pressed the button for the street. All the way down, he forced himself not to think about anything bad. He refused to think about not being able to perform. About losing Lee's friendship.

Yeah, right.

"WHAT'S WRONG?"

Trevor stared at Lee's two suitcases, both of which could hold enough clothes for a week, then at his own small overnight bag. He shook his head, but refrained from comment as he loaded the car. Lee got in the passenger seat, wondering if she should take off her sweater.

She'd chosen a simple outfit, a white scoop-necked T-shirt and slim-legged jeans, for the trip—after trying on pretty much everything in her closet. Underneath the T-shirt she wore her new beige Wonder bra, and she felt as though she were a walking pair of boobs on legs. She could serve hors d'oeuvres on her cleavage. He couldn't help but notice. Not while he sat so close. The drive would last at least two hours, and she didn't want to be self-conscious the whole time. On the other hand, maybe when he got a load of her enhanced figure, it would help him get into the mood. If he got all sexy, then she was bound to forget her nerves and get into the mood, too.

The trunk of the BMW slammed shut, and she quickly took off the gray cardigan, tossing it into the back seat just as he opened his door.

She sat back, trying to look casual, as he got in beside her. He smiled, she smiled back. He started the car. She kept on smiling. He put the car in gear, and eased into traffic. It occurred to Lee that her perception of how she looked must be exaggerated. Trevor didn't even—

The car swerved all the way to the other side of the road, and Trevor cursed as he fought to get it back in the right lane.

Okay, so it wasn't exaggerated. He kept looking at

her chest, then the road, then her chest. She felt as if she were at a tennis match.

Finally, he pulled up to a red light and turned to face her. "I— You—"

"Don't worry. They won't bite."

"I'm not so sure."

"Wonder bra," she said.

"Wonder bra?" he echoed, his focus now entirely on the front of her shirt.

"Yes. Same boobs, different bra."

"God bless modern technology," he said.

Lee's smile began to hurt, and more than anything she wanted to put her sweater back on. Which was nuts, because the whole reason she'd worn the bra was to get this reaction.

Trevor cleared his throat, then snapped his gaze forward as the light turned green. She saw his Adam's apple bob several times, and a very slight sheen of sweat on his brow.

They drove in silence for a while, fighting the evening traffic. It was after seven, and the worst of rush hour was over, but in Manhattan, there was no good time to drive. Trevor was very good at darting and weaving. He even made a couple of cabdrivers honk. Lee used the time to relax. Or at least to try. She took a deep breath, and let it out. She thought of the old seaport village of Mystic, and how beautiful and peaceful the weekend would be. No good. She still felt her adrenaline pump with vigor throughout her body. All she could do was try harder.

They got on the highway and Lee focused on the

sound of the tires. She knew she should say something. In all the years she'd known Trevor, they'd never had an awkward silence. Ever. Maybe one of the gang would call. That would break the silence. But no, everyone had been given strict orders not to call.

So she just stared ahead, watching the taillights of a minivan.

"What's that you're humming?"

Lee jumped, surprised by Trevor's voice. "What?"

"That song. I know it, but I can't place it."

She hadn't realized she'd been humming, but as soon as he said it, she knew what it was. "'It's A Small World.'"

Trevor looked at her as if she were nuts. "Yeah, I heard that song was making a comeback."

"I'll be quiet. I promise."

"It's too late. It's already in my head." He leaned forward and turned on the radio. Something classical came on first, but he pressed the buttons until he found a soft-rock station.

The newest cut from Hootie and the Blowfish came on and Trevor started singing with it. Never one to be shy, he sang with as much gusto and emotion as Hootie himself. Unfortunately, Trevor's voice sounded more like an actual blowfish. A tone-deaf blowfish at that.

But she couldn't complain. He enjoyed himself so much when he sang, he always had. Poor guy would have killed to get into a band, or even a choir, but no one would have him. So he used the shower, or the car, and if someone happened to be in earshot, he didn't even blink.

Oddly, his painful serenade comforted her, and for the first time since she'd gotten in the car, Lee felt herself relax. Her shoulders first, then her neck. She moved so that her side wasn't pressing into the door handle and crossed her ankles.

Trevor kept on singing.

Of course, she thought about what they were about to do. But the panic had left her somewhere around exit fifty-seven. How could sleeping with Trevor be anything but wonderful? There wasn't a shy bone in his body. No self-consciousness at all, except of course when he was asked to drop his pants for her perusal. She had the feeling if she'd pressed him on that, he'd have done it for her eventually. It didn't matter now. She had pretty underwear, and that was half the battle. He'd already shown her that he wasn't immune to the Wonder bra, and with a little luck and a quick turn of a light switch, she'd make it under the covers unscathed.

The song ended and Trevor gave her a luscious grin. "That's better."

"For who? Now I've got your voice in my head."

"It's your own fault. Oh, hey, listen."

Lee smiled as the first chords of "Let's Give 'Em Something To Talk About" came on the radio. "Oh, my God. Do you remember—"

"That pizza?"

"The pizza? What about that wine? What was it, Strawberry Ripple?"

"Yeah, oh, man." Trevor shook his head and she could see her own memories in his face. "That was the first night we really talked."

"All night," she said, the conversation so clear to her that it might have taken place eight days ago instead of eight years.

Trevor looked at her, his grin fading. "I had the hots for you like nobody's business."

"You did?"

"Why do you think I had the pizza box on my lap all night?"

To say she was surprised was an understatement. "Are we talking about the same night? Bonnie Raitt on the CD, pizza with extra cheese and pepperoni? Midterms staring at us like a firing squad?"

"Oh, yeah. That was me. And it was you, and I was a goner."

Lee was stunned. Not just simply stunned, but down to the very core shaken. He'd had a thing for her? All the way back in college? It didn't make sense. "Why didn't you say anything?"

He looked in the rearview mirror, then at the road. She wanted to hurry him up, to understand how she'd seemingly misunderstood the entire gist of one of the most important nights of her life.

"I was going to say something," he said, "but you'd just broken up with Frank Baskin, and you were so vulnerable."

"Frank Baskin. I haven't even thought about him in years."

"He's come to my mind several times. If I recall, he was the prototype."

"Excuse me?"

"He was wealthy, handsome, bright and so selfish he wouldn't spit on you if you were on fire."

"Oh, yeah. That Frank Baskin."

"You blamed yourself. For everything. Remember that?"

She did. Her self-esteem had been so low in college, at least in the beginning. But after she'd moved into her dorm room with Katy and Susan, and met Peter, Ben and Trevor, that had changed. Especially after she'd met Trevor.

She'd started listening to him, and after a while, she'd started believing him. He'd told her that she didn't have to take any crap from anyone. That she deserved to be loved for who she was. And that she was in charge of her own fate. Some of it had stuck. She'd become a stockbroker even though her father had wanted her to be an English teacher. She'd never compromised ethically in a business situation, even when all around her were temptations that would try a saint.

The only part that she'd never bought was the part about being loved. The idea that there was nothing wrong with her when it came to men. Trevor had given it his best, but finally he'd given up in the face of far too much evidence to the contrary. She'd still managed to hook up with Josh, and get her heart broken. "I'm still confused. I *was* vulnerable. Clingy. You could have had me in a hot second."

"Gee, thanks for sharing that," Trevor said.

"Tell me why you didn't tell me."

"I didn't tell you because I didn't want to take advantage of you. I didn't want to do what every guy would have done. It was more important for me to be your friend."

"Oh."

"And yet," he said, "that lesson seems to have been lost somewhere, eh?"

"No, I don't think so. I think you're the best thing that ever happened to me."

"Ditto, kid. Even without Strawberry Ripple, you still make me crazy. I still want you enough to lift a deep-dish pizza box. And I still value your friendship more than anything else in the world."

Lee had to swallow several times before she could speak. "So you're saying you don't want to..."

"No. I'm saying it's okay if *you* don't."

"Even after you've seen my Wonder breasts?"

He smiled. "Well, I don't know. They are pretty outstanding."

"And that's not all. There're panties to match."

"You're making this harder than it needs to be. No pun intended."

"Ha."

"Ha."

"Trevor?"

"Yep?"

"It's not a thong."

"Pardon?"

"The underwear. They're not thongs. I'm sorry."

He laughed, then touched her knee. "It's okay. I forgive you."

"If I'd known you were going to be this sweet, I would have gotten the thongs."

He sniffed loudly, only slightly mocking her. "That's the nicest thing anyone's ever said to me."

She smiled, reached for his hand and brought it up to her lips. She kissed his palm, savoring the Trevor smell, then put his hand right back where it had been on her leg.

Maybe she didn't have to turn out the lights, after all. Maybe Trevor had always known exactly what she looked like.

7

THEY REACHED Mystic at a quarter to ten. Trevor hadn't been to the Carlisle Inn for years, and the place was even more beautiful than he remembered. Once a tavern built in 1740, the owner had meticulously restored the building itself, and decorated the guest rooms with period furnishings.

"This is gorgeous," Lee said.

"Have you ever been to Mystic?"

She shook her head. "The only thing I know about Mystic is that it's supposed to have good pizza."

Trevor laughed as he parked the car in a small parking lot adjacent to the main building. "Come on. Let's get inside. I don't know about you, but I'm tired." He stepped out into the cool night air. He'd been right to bring his jacket. And to book the room with the fireplace.

"Do you smell that?" Lee asked.

He looked across the top of the car to see her take in a great breath of air. "What?"

"The ocean. I can actually smell the seaweed. This was a wonderful idea."

"Was it?" He regretted the words the second they were out of his mouth. Lee seemed surprised, as if she didn't expect him to still have doubts.

"If nothing else, we're away from the city," she said, but too brightly. "No phones, no cabs, no jack-hammers."

He walked to the trunk, popping it open with the remote on his key chain. "Absolutely right. And I think you're going to like it here."

Lee took one of her suitcases while Trevor carried in the other, along with his overnight bag. He'd called ahead and warned the proprietor that they would be arriving late, and from the porch light, it looked like they weren't going to have any problems. He really wanted things to go smoothly. The whole weekend seemed as fragile as thin ice. Lee was nervous. She tried to hide it, but he could tell. The way she nibbled on her lower lip. The humming. He wished he could ease her fears, but the truth was, he was just as nervous.

As they walked up the gravel path, the crunch of their shoes loud in the still night, Trevor thought again about his confession to Lee. He'd made it sound light, sexual, as if that night in the dorm wasn't a particularly big deal. Which wasn't the truth.

First, it had been more adoration than love. He'd had a crush, that's all. In time, it had eased, turning into the warmest friendship of his life, so why bring it up? The whole purpose of this plan of hers was to free themselves of the baggage that always accompanied love. The neediness, the games, the jealousy. The last thing he wanted to do was veer the conversation in that direction.

Lee held the door open for him, and he led her into the front room of the great old building. It was like stepping back in time.

Wooden walls with eighteenth-century paintings graced the entryway, and just beyond that was the living room. The smell of freshly baked bread mingled with the scent of spice, filling him immediately with a sense of calm. The huge hearth that dominated the living room housed a well-tended fire. A young couple sat on an overstuffed couch, so close together he could hardly tell where the boy left off and the girl began.

"Good evening."

Trevor turned from the fire and the lovers to greet the hostess. She looked as cozy as the accommodations, plump, gray-haired, smiling warmly. "I'm Hester," she said, "and you must be Mr. Templeton."

"Yes," he said, putting down the suitcases to shake her hand. "And this is Ms. Phillips."

Hester welcomed Lee, then handed Trevor a registration card. "Don't bother about this now. It's late, and I'm sure you two want to get settled in. Just fill this out and bring it down with you tomorrow morning. Come, let me show you to your room."

Lee grinned at Trevor, and he couldn't help but smile back. They had truly crossed the threshold into an otherworldly place. The smells, the warm air, the antiques, were all as far away from midtown Manhattan as they could be.

They walked down a portrait-lined hallway, until

Hester stopped at the last door. She opened it with a key, not an electronic card, thank goodness, and stood aside to let them pass.

Lee's sharp intake of breath told him the room was perfect even before he stepped inside. Once he joined her, he nodded. Everything *was* perfect. A fire crackled, the love seat in front of it had a brightly colored afghan tossed over the arm, making it seem as welcoming as an old friend. The bottle of champagne he'd ordered sat nestled in a tall ice bucket.

He looked at Lee, then back at the love seat, and her image came to him as clearly as a photograph. Lee, languid on the couch, naked and beautiful. Her skin aglow with the reflections of the fire, her smile as inviting as her posture.

Trevor jerked his gaze away, only to find himself staring at the bed. It was a huge four-poster, with a white canopy, big fluffy pillows and a goose-down comforter. Now his mind's eye pictured Lee there, propped against the pillows, her auburn hair framing her face. Her body stretched out in all its glory, naked and—

"It's gorgeous," Lee said.

"Oh, yes," he whispered, the image still shimmering before him.

"It's also quiet." Hester's voice shattered the illusion but it still took a moment to get his equilibrium back. He'd had no idea his imagination could be so vivid, or that it could cause such an immediate physical impact. His jeans felt tighter than was comfortable. He needed a pizza box.

"There's no one in the room next door," Hester continued as she walked past the big bed. "Here's the bathroom." She waited for Lee to take a look. "It's one of my favorite places in the house."

Trevor realized he was still holding the suitcases. He put down the bags and followed Lee into the incredible room. Large, with an oversize claw-foot tub against one wall, a pedestal sink against the other, and a commode gently hidden behind a lace curtain, it was a room built with comfort in mind. Candles lined two shelves, all lit, creating intricate shadows on the walls.

He saw Lee in the tub, one leg hooked over the edge, beads of moisture glistening on her chest. Tendrils of hair teasing her neck. *Oh, damn.*

"Now I'll leave you two to get unpacked. Breakfast is served from nine to ten-thirty. I'm afraid there's no room service tonight, but if you find you're missing something, let me know in the morning, and I'll do what I can."

"Thank you, Hester," Lee said, taking the woman's hand as they headed for the door. "It's perfect."

"I like to think so," the older woman said. "Have a lovely evening."

Trevor slowly turned away from the tub, and mumbled a goodbye. Lee had moved to the fireplace, and now stood staring at the flames. Was she thinking about what came next? About turning all the images into real flesh and heat?

She turned to him, a mysterious smile on her moistened lips. "You know what it feels like?"

"What?" he said, walking toward her, amazed at the connection between them, certain she felt the anticipation just as strongly as he did.

"It's like we're in the holodeck on the *Enterprise*."

Trevor stopped. He laughed out loud, not just at her incredibly weird logic, but at his own romanticism. Connection. Right. Two peas in a pod. He laughed again. "It's supposed to make you feel like you're in the past, not the future."

"I know. But it feels surreal. This place. Us."

He nodded, then headed for the champagne. He didn't know about Lee, but he certainly could use a drink.

"I can't help picturing..."

He stopped again. "Worf?"

She grinned. "Nope. I'll take a glass of that, please. I can't help picturing all the couples who've been here before us. It's not like a hotel room. It's so much more personal here."

"I know," he said, putting the towel that had circled the bottle over the cork. "That's why I thought you'd like it." He pulled until he felt the cork pop, then poured the bubbly into the two crystal flutes Hester had put on the occasional table.

"Thanks."

Lee had come up right beside him, and when he handed her the glass, their fingers brushed. At once, as if the touch had been a checkered flag, the images raced back into his head, one on top of the other, but all of them with her in the center.

"To friendship," she said, raising the glass.

"To friendship," he echoed, making sure the rim of his glass touched its mate gently. He drank, watching her bring the crystal to her lips, mesmerized by the movement in her throat. His gaze went lower, to the lush mounds of her breasts, made so prominent by her new lingerie. The urge to touch her grew until it hurt so much he had to walk away.

He occupied his hands by getting out his shaving kit, and occupied his mind by reciting Babe Ruth's batting stats. The painful condition of his groin eased with the activity and he let out a calming breath as he headed for the bathroom.

"So, you want to go to bed?" she asked softly, just as he reached the door.

All his hard work went to hell in a handbasket. He was instantly aroused, painfully aware of her proximity, and his desire. "Sure," he said, his voice as casual as a stroll in the park. "I'll just be a minute."

He shut the door, went to the sink, and turned on the water. But he didn't wash. He stared at himself in the mirror. His image wasn't clear with the room being so dark, but still he was able to see his eyes. Yep, he looked as desperate as he felt. It wasn't like any other time, with any other woman. Even his first time hadn't been this full of anxiety. Half of him wanted to call the whole thing off and drive back to New York, but the other half, the lower half, wanted nothing more than to hold her in his arms. To learn all her secrets. To fulfill a wish made eight long years ago.

He leaned down, bringing a handful of warm water to his face. The trick of tonight was going to be listening. Paying careful attention, and letting Lee set the pace. It would require superhuman effort, but it had to be played that way. If she changed her mind at any stage of the game, he'd smile and tell her it was fine. The important thing was their overall relationship. No way he was going to leave this inn with any awkwardness between them. He'd fight for this friendship, and he'd win. Whether they were lovers or not.

LEE LIFTED her negligee out of the suitcase. Black, floor length, with lace around the bodice, it was the prettiest nightgown she'd ever owned. It made her look exotic and sensual, and she knew Trevor would like it a lot. The thing was, she wasn't ready for him to see it at all.

Despite the wonderful talk on the way here, the perfectly gorgeous room, the fire and the champagne, she was still stuck in doubt. She'd convinced herself that once she got here, once she'd crossed the point of no return, that all her uncertainties and fears were going to vanish.

They hadn't.

Oh, boy, they hadn't. If she thought that all they were going to do was talk and cuddle, she'd be the most relaxed woman in New England. But that's not what they were here to do. This was about sex. She'd wanted it to be about sex. Sex was good. Sex between friends should be even better. Sex with Trevor would be the best of the best. So, what was her problem?

She folded the negligee over her arm, then got out her makeup kit and put it on the bed. She wouldn't be needing anything else, so she zipped up her suitcase and stashed it in the closet.

As the door to the bathroom opened, she answered her own question. Her problem wasn't about her having sex with Trevor, it was about Trevor having sex with her.

She'd been nervous about making love before, but never like this. Always before, there hadn't been much to lose if things didn't work out. But with Trevor? What if he didn't get turned on once they were in bed? What if he hated the way she kissed? What if she was too loud, and it turned him off?

What if she made a run for it, and called him from New York?

Too late. Trevor smiled at her, and nodded toward the bathroom. "It's all yours."

How could he be so calm? He looked as if this were just another night, with nothing at all at stake. Didn't he care that this might change everything?

He headed toward the bed, unbuttoning his shirt as he went. She hurried into the bathroom and shut the door behind her.

He was taking off his clothes. Right now. Right out there. She was going to take her clothes off. Right now. Right in here.

The bathroom was large, and the tub looked roomy. Maybe she'd just stay here for the night.

No. No, no, no. She was the one who'd asked him. She'd practically had to twist his arm to do this. She couldn't back out now.

Before she could change her mind, she got undressed and tossed her T-shirt and jeans onto the edge of the tub. Next, the Wonder bra came off, and she immediately wanted to put it on again. God, she felt so droopy without the material thrusting her up and out. But she couldn't exactly wear the bra with the nightgown. He'd notice.

She slipped the gown over her head, and then she took off her panties. Slowly, she turned to the mirror, squinting at her reflection. It wasn't so bad. She opened her eyes all the way. She looked okay. She'd never make the cover of *Vogue*, but she didn't need to put a paper bag over her head, either.

The black satin made her skin look delicate and smooth. The lace around the bodice accentuated her breasts. She smoothed her hands down her hips. It was going to be fine.

She got her toothbrush out, and her mouthwash. Then she saw his toothbrush, still wet, neatly atop his black shaving kit. She'd seen his toothbrush a hundred times before in his bathroom at home. She'd never given it a second thought. Now, it seemed the height of intimacy. It had just been in his mouth, and he'd used it so he'd have minty fresh breath when he kissed her. She needed to talk to Katy. Susan would know what to do. Where was her phone, and who the hell thought that banning phone calls for the weekend was a good idea?

She was officially on her own, and she hated it. With a shaking hand, she put the toothpaste on her brush, and then it hit her. She wasn't alone. Her best friend in the whole world was right outside. She could tell him she was nervous, and he'd understand. The fact was, she could go outside right this second and tell him she wanted to call the whole thing off. It was Trevor, after all. Trevor, who knew her insecurities, her faults, her insanity, and loved her anyway.

The anxiety that had plagued her for hours slipped away in a wave of relief. She'd been making herself crazy for nothing. It was Trevor. Just Trevor. No matter what, it would be okay.

She brushed her teeth, used her mouthwash, took off her makeup, brushed her hair. All the while remembering that nothing could possibly go wrong. Not with Trevor at her side.

After one last look in the mirror, she gathered her clothes, took a deep breath and opened the bathroom door.

The fire was the only light in the room. Trevor was already in bed, sitting, his back propped up by the big pillows. He was in pajamas, and she felt grateful for that. If he'd been naked, it might have been scary, but pajamas were practically clothes.

She went to the closet, threw her things inside, and turned back to face the bed. She wondered how much he could see in this light. And if he liked what he saw.

"Oh, God," he said.

"What's wrong?"

"You're so beautiful."

The words seemed to float over to her, buoyed by the shadows that danced on the walls. She believed him. Completely. Moving toward him, feeling his gaze on her, she wanted to say something appropriate, meaningful. She wanted him to know how much she cared about him, and how just knowing he was here gave her the courage to keep walking. But the words didn't come together. When she reached his side, and he tossed back the covers, the words didn't seem so important anymore.

She slid right next to him, until her side pressed against his. He covered her with the blanket, and then he moved his hand to hers and gave her a gentle squeeze. "Are you nervous?" she asked.

"A little," he said, but the way his voice cracked told her he wasn't being entirely truthful.

"I am, too," she admitted. "Sort of."

"We don't have to do anything."

"I know."

His hand moved, and she felt his thumb stroke her palm. It was a lovely, light touch.

"Do you want to?" she whispered.

"I do, if you do."

"I do," she agreed. "I think."

"You think?"

She nodded, finally gathering the courage to look

at him. His concern for her was so obvious it made her chest tighten. He smiled, and she loved what that did to his face. It was a beautiful face, not just because of his classic good looks, but because it was full of kindness. Because it was filled with love.

"Tell you what," he said, releasing her hand. "Let's scoot down."

After they were lying flat, he sort of turned her on her side then he curled up behind her in the spoon position. His arm went around her waist and she could feel his warm breath on her neck. "We'll just lie here for a while," he suggested. "We'll talk."

"I like this," she said, getting used to the feel of his body so close. His chest on her back. His arm gently squeezing her. Letting her know that he was in no rush to do the deed. Or maybe that he didn't want to do it at all. She felt a little disappointed, but not much. It was probably for the best. Actually, she felt relieved. The pressure was off, and she could relax.

But then she shifted.... It took a minute to realize what pressed against her hip. She held her breath, making sure that what she felt was what she thought she felt.

Oh, yes. It was. He wasn't spooning because he didn't want her. It was because she'd hesitated.

Now she understood. His body had told her what his words couldn't. He wanted her. He was ready. But it was up to her to make the first move.

Now, she had to decide. All she had to do was reach down and touch him. Turn over and kiss him. She wanted to. Her body's reaction to him was a dead giveaway. The tightness in her stomach, the ache in her breasts. The way she needed to squeeze her legs together.

All systems were go. Everything was as perfect as it could be. Nothing was stopping her.

Except the fact that she knew, with all her heart, that this was completely wrong.

8

"WHAT'S WRONG?"

Lee hadn't said a word. She hadn't moved, or even breathed, and yet Trevor had felt the difference. She didn't want to tell him, but he'd know anyway. "I'm not sure how to explain it," she said. "But I, uh, I'm not... Maybe we shouldn't..."

"Make love?"

"Uh-huh."

She waited for him to say something, but he didn't. She shifted her attention to his body, hoping she could read him as astutely as he'd read her. His hand didn't tighten on her waist, his legs didn't shift. And the most obvious sign of his willingness to move ahead didn't shrink. The only thing that changed at all was his breath on her neck. It slowed, and for a moment, it stopped all together. After several seconds, she felt him exhale.

"Are you mad at me?" she asked, praying she hadn't done irreparable damage with this crazy scheme. The trip up and the time they'd spent in the room had shown her more clearly than ever before that Trevor was the most important person in her life. Relationships come and go, but Trevor...he'd be hers forever, if she didn't screw things up.

"Of course not," he said. "I'd be lying if I said I wasn't a little disappointed, but I'll get over it."

"Why?"

"Why will I get over it? Because I'm not twelve."

"No, that's not what I meant. Why are you disappointed?"

"Uh, isn't that, um, obvious?"

She felt him shift his hips, reminding her again that despite his very kind acquiescence, his body had been ready for takeoff when she'd pushed the abort switch. "I meant, are you disappointed because we're not having sex, or because you wanted the relationship to, you know, change?"

He grew still again, except for his hand. She felt it move on her waist, rubbing the satin nightgown in small circles just above her belly button. "Yes," he said.

"Yes?"

"I think it's a little late to deny I was looking forward to making love. But I'd also given the relationship thing a lot of thought. The idea of being with you, like this...knowing that we could be even closer. I don't know. It seemed like a good thing."

"What about the scary parts?"

"Yeah, I thought about those, too. But then I looked at the relationships I've had. The family I come from. Marriage only works for a tiny percentage of people, who obviously are born with some special sort of marriage gene. No way I got that. In my family, the only people who had any happiness at all were the ones who stayed single."

"I didn't realize there were any people in your family who'd stayed single."

"Yeah, I've got an aunt in Quebec who never married. Of course, she's a lesbian, and she's been with her partner for over ten years. Hey! Maybe that's the trick. I need to become a lesbian."

"You don't have the qualifications," Lee said, grinning.

"I can fake it."

"Some things you can't fake."

"Damn. I knew there had to be a catch."

She turned around, even though she hated to move from the incredibly comforting position. But she needed to see his face. To make sure things were okay. Once she'd settled, she lay just as close, but facing him, their heads both on the same pillow, their knees touching.

He smiled, and she felt better immediately. Grateful for the firelight, she could see he wasn't hiding anything. That he still loved her, even though she'd backed out at the last minute.

Trevor looked at her for a few seconds, his gaze traveling over her face patiently, as if he would be tested on the details. When he finished his perusal of her chin, he looked back up into her eyes. "There's something I want to say. Before we go back to the way we were."

"What's that?" she asked, her tummy tightening in apprehension. Or excitement. She wasn't sure which.

He reached up and stroked her cheek with the

back of his hand. The touch so light, it was more than a caress. Somehow, it was reverent, as if he meant to honor her.

She closed her eyes, soaking in the exquisite feel of his skin on hers. Fighting the quiver that started deep inside and spread to her most vulnerable spots.

"You are the most beautiful woman I've ever seen," he whispered. "Not just because your face was made by angels, but because you make me feel so damn good. You make me laugh and you make me think. I'm more generous when I'm around you, and you've taught me not to take everything so damn seriously. But mostly, I think you're beautiful because you have the kindest heart in the world."

"Oh, Trev—"

"I'm not finished."

She looked at him, the tears in her eyes blurring his face, but not so much that she couldn't see the awesome tenderness in his gaze.

"I think making love to you would be as close to heaven as a man can get. But I also know that I'd rather cut off my own arm than do anything that would make you uncomfortable. The thing is, I love you, kiddo. I trust you."

She sighed, unable to speak for the lump in her throat. She touched the back of his head, then leaned over and kissed him gently on the mouth.

The softness of his lips held her there.

His quiet moan made her deepen the kiss.

What happened to her insides changed everything.

Surrendering herself to the moment, to the rightness of her new decision, to the forces that drew her inexorably to his arms, she tasted him, using the tip of her tongue to tease his lips. He moaned again, this time in pleasure as he understood her intentions. He kissed her back, tasting her in return, moving closer, using his hand on her back to bring her to him. Then he hesitated, leaned back just enough to see her. "Are you sure?" he whispered, his voice low and gruff with desire.

"Completely," she whispered back. To show him that she meant it, she reached down below the covers, touched the front of his silk pajamas at his waist, then moved her hand down until she found his erection. She took her time exploring, not reaching inside his pajamas, just feeling the shape and the size of him.

It wasn't awkward at all. Not even for a second. The last of her doubts were swept away at that moment.

He closed his eyes and moaned once more, and she smiled, pleased beyond reason that he enjoyed her touch so much. That his reaction to her was so impressive.

It wasn't enough. She wanted more than to feel him through the material. She wanted to see him. To taste him. And more than anything, she wanted him inside her.

Her heart thudded in her chest as she slipped her fingers inside his pajamas and touched his heated flesh. Smooth as silk, hot as the fire, and hard as steel.

So thick she could just circle him with her hand, and when she stroked him to the base, he grew even thicker.

"Oh, Lee, you can't know. It feels..."

"Tell me."

He looked at her with the passion in his gaze so electric she felt a jolt in her soul. "I'll show you," he whispered. He reached down and pulled her hand away, then he slipped out of bed, and took his pajamas off.

Lee's gaze lingered on his chest for a moment, at once so familiar and yet so new. So different now, knowing it was hers to kiss, to stroke. Then she looked down, to the part of him she'd never seen before. To the strong muscles of his lower stomach, the tight hips, and to his erection, so powerfully male it made her gasp.

She wanted him as she'd never wanted any man before. It was a totally unique experience, something she'd never anticipated, not even when she'd tried so hard to imagine this moment.

Her love for him swelled, matched only by her trust. She knew without hesitation that this incredible man would never hurt her. Never.

She tossed the covers back and moved closer to him. Looking up, she reveled in his beauty, and in his smile. Then she reached out once more to touch him, guiding him to her mouth.

He took in a sharp breath of air as her lips touched his silky head. Kissing him lightly, savoring his clean, masculine scent, she moved slowly, unwilling

Play the

"LAS V

3 FRE

FREE GIFTS!

1. Pull back all 3 tabs on t
   see what we have for yo
   FREE!

2. Send back this card and
   novels. These books ha
   $4.25 each in Canada,

3. There's no catch. You'r
   nothing — ZERO — fo
   any minimum number

4. The fact is thousands o
   Harlequin Reader Servi
   they like getting the be
   and they love our disc

5. We hope that after rece
   subscriber. But the ch
   all! So why not take us
   You'll be glad you did!

▼ DETACH AND MAIL TODAY ▼

Play the
"LAS VEGAS"
Game

PEEL BACK HERE▶
PEEL BACK HERE▶
PEEL BACK HERE▶

YES! I have pulled back the 3 tabs. Please send me all the free Harlequin Temptation® books and the gift for which I qualify. I understand that I am under no obligation to purchase any books, as explained on the back and opposite page.

342 HDL CTLD   **142 HDL CTKZ**

Name _____ (Please Print Clearly) _____

Address _____ Apt. _____

City _____ State/Prov. _____ Zip/Postal Code _____

GET 2 FREE BOOKS & A FREE MYSTERY GIFT!

GET 2 FREE BOOKS!

GET 1 FREE BOOK!

TRY AGAIN!

Offer limited to one per household and not valid to current Harlequin Temptation® subscribers. All orders subject to approval.

(H-T-11/99)

PRINTED IN U.S.A.

The Harlequin Reader Service®—Here's how it works:

If offer card is missing write to: Harlequin Reader Service, 3010 Walden Ave., P.O. Box 1867, Buffalo, NY 14240-1867

BUSINESS REPLY MAIL
FIRST-CLASS MAIL   PERMIT NO. 717   BUFFALO, NY

POSTAGE WILL BE PAID BY ADDRESSEE

HARLEQUIN READER SERVICE
3010 WALDEN AVE
PO BOX 1867
BUFFALO NY 14240-9952

NO POSTAGE
NECESSARY
IF MAILED
IN THE
UNITED STATES

to rush any part of this. He hadn't let out his breath
as she licked him in a circle, then took the crown in
her mouth. As she flicked her tongue, sucking hard
at the same time, he finally let his breath go, sending
an almost painful groan with it.

She heard her name, soft and shaky. Gripping him
with her hand, she pulled him into her mouth. Then
with a steady rhythm that matched her heartbeat,
she moved her tongue up and down the length of
him. She pulled back, pausing to use the tip of her
tongue, then moved down again, as far as she could
go.

Her eyes fluttered closed as she moved to cup him
from below, amazed at the uniqueness of his body,
so incredibly different from her own, and so perfect.

He touched the back of her head, and for a moment she thought it was to encourage her, but then
she realized he wanted her to stop. Puzzled, she
pulled back, letting go with her hand and her lips.

"I want to see you," he said. "Please."

She nodded, then shifted her legs to the end of the
bed so she could stand next to him. Reaching for the
bottom of her nightgown, he held out his hand to
stop her once more. His fingers took over, bunching
the black satin in his large fists and lifting the material slowly upward.

She felt the cool air on her legs, and her thighs, and
then her stomach. He paused, glancing down, then
continued at the same measured pace.

When the bottom of the gown reached her breasts,
she thought about how she'd been so worried an

hour ago. Now, she realized all that fretting was for nothing. She wanted him to see her. Flaws and all. It didn't matter. Nothing mattered but this incredible closeness. They'd jumped off the cliff together, not knowing where they would land. Instead of a jarring crash, they'd found a soft cushion of love and wonder.

His sigh told her all she needed to know. That he loved the way she looked, just as she loved his body. She raised her arms and he lifted the gown the rest of the way, then tossed it on the end of the bed.

"You're stunning," he said. "More beautiful than I ever imagined."

She smiled, touched that he was looking into her eyes as he said the flattering words. "I feel pretty," she said.

"I'm glad. I just wish you could feel what I do. See what I see."

She touched his chest with the palm of her hand, then rubbed his soft skin, enjoying the contradiction created by hard muscles that lay beneath.

He kissed her, encircling her shoulders with both arms, bringing her close. Her hand stilled, caught between them, but she didn't care. His kiss took all her thoughts, and as she felt him tease her with his talented tongue, she had to squeeze her legs together to try to ease the insistent ache.

As if he'd read her mind, he broke the kiss and turned her so she could lie down. He followed, waited until she'd scooted to the middle of the mattress, then kissed her once more.

His hand found her breast and she shivered with that first touch. He cupped her gently, then ran his palm over her erect nipple. Just as the featherlight touch became unbearably sweet, he moved his mouth to the very same spot, taking her nipple between his teeth, sucking her flesh hard and sharp.

Her back arched, and her eyes closed. The sensation was overwhelming; so pleasurable it was almost too much. Almost. He toyed with her, using his tongue and his lips and his breath, each move more exquisite than the last. The pressure in her core built unbearably, the tension stiffened her body as if she'd been shocked by a hundred volts.

He let go of her right nipple, and found her left. He repeated his ministrations, only this time, knowing what she was in for, it was impossible to be still.

Her hips moved up and down on the bed, the unselfconscious prelude to what she wanted more than her next breath. She found his hand and guided it down so he could feel her body's reaction to his touch. His tongue stopped making the tiny little swirls on her nipple the moment he touched her. Stroking her softly, he parted her lips with his fingertips. Without a pause, he found the jutting flesh that so controlled her passion. Then the swirls began again, only this time, with his finger.

She moaned, drowning in a sea of pleasure. She was going to come, she could feel it start deep in her groin. His movements grew quicker, quicker, and then he stopped, and she cried out in dismay. As soon as she saw where he was, her objection changed to anticipation. He'd slipped silently down the bed. She'd been so caught up in her own sensations she hadn't even noticed.

She heard a soft rip, and saw that he'd gotten a condom packet. He took out the circle of thin rubber and then she closed her eyes.

A moment later, he lifted her legs gently, moving them apart as he got comfortable. His palms traced the insides of her thighs, and then his thumbs met at her juncture. Once more, he opened her, and his hot breath hit her only seconds before he captured her bud between his lips.

She cried out, grabbing the sheets and lifting them from the mattress. Her hips moved up and stayed there as he did unspeakably wonderful things with his tongue.

It started again, her climax. Deep inside, making her tense, making her insane. Her head shook from side to side. She stopped breathing. But he never stopped. The pressure increased as he narrowed his focus to that one tiny spot, and then she jerked with a climax that rocked her body.

He stayed with her as tremor after tremor hit her. Then he stopped, sat up, captured her legs just below her knees, and she felt his thick heat surge inside her. She came a second time as he thrust home. He filled her completely, finally easing the ache that had threatened to drive her mad.

Lifting her legs to his shoulders, he angled down so he could enter her more fully. His hips slammed into her roughly, the energy behind them as feral and basic as primeval man, as urgent and powerful as a force of nature.

She opened her eyes to find him staring at her, unblinking, his face a mask of lust, his gaze so hot it scorched her. He never wavered, never glanced away. Just thrust into her over and over, the pace increasing as the tension in his body made the cords of his neck stand out.

Trembling, squeezing, she milked him, wanting to draw him deeper and deeper inside. He moved her legs around his waist and she clung to him with all her might.

He was going to come. She could see it in his face, feel it in his pulsing rhythm. She thought he was going to scream, but instead, he swept down and kissed her, hard. She kissed him back, waiting for his moment of release.

When it came, he cried out, but he didn't break the kiss. She felt the air from his lungs, the release of his energy, enter her like a shaft of white light which brought her to climax once more.

They came together. It lasted a long time. Wave after wave of jolting pleasure, of tightening and relaxing, only to tense again.

Finally, the earth slowed to its normal pace, leaving the two of them damp, bedraggled and utterly spent.

He finally broke the kiss. But before he moved away, he smiled, and it melted her heart. She'd never dared hope that it would be like this. Her imagination wasn't good enough.

This was so much more, it scared her.

TREVOR EASED onto his back trying to make his pulse slow and his breathing steady. He knew he had to go to the bathroom to clean up, but he couldn't move. Not yet. Every ounce of energy had drained away, and now that he was lying down, he thought it was very possible that he'd never move again.

Well, maybe not. If Lee wanted a second helping, he'd manage. Although, it was going to take him a while to recover enough to speak, let alone perform again.

"You have some nerve," Lee said.

He lifted his head an inch so he could see her face. It was too much effort, and he fell back to the pillow. "Why's that?"

"Because you never told me."

"Told you what?"

"That you could win gold medals in the bedroom triple crown."

He smiled. "Yeah, I should have mentioned it. Sorry."

She pinched him on the side, and he had just enough energy to yelp.

"You kept some secrets yourself, missy."

"Oh, yeah?"

"Uh-huh."

"Never. I told you over and over that I was the hottest thing since sliced bread. You never paid attention."

"You liar. You never said any such thing."

"I know, but it sounded good, didn't it?"

"It's true, you know. You are the hottest thing since sliced bread."

She found his hand and squeezed his fingers. "Speaking of bread..."

"Hungry?"

"Ravenous."

"But doesn't that mean one of us has to move?"

"Unless you have a peanut-butter-and-jelly sandwich hidden in your pillow."

"Damn, I didn't bring that pillow."

"Then yes, it means one of us has to move."

He sighed. "I guess I'm the one, huh?"

"Oh, you're so perceptive. I just love that about you."

He grinned. Rolled over. Looked at her all naked and shiny, right there next to him. He could still smell her, and the scent intoxicated him. Made him stir, which was quite unbelievable, as he'd been almost sure he'd never have the use of that particular organ again.

"There's fruit and chocolate in my floral suitcase," she said.

"That's not what I'm hungry for."

Her eyes widened. "You're kidding."

He sighed. "Only slightly. But after we eat..."

"Oh, goody," she said. "You know how I feel about dessert."

As he listened to her rich laugh, the silliness of their conversation ebbed, and in its place a deep sense of calm settled in his chest. "This was good," he said.

"I know," she said, as suddenly serious as he.

"I didn't expect it would be like this."

"Me, neither."

"What do you suppose it means?"

"I'm not certain," she said, catching his gaze and holding it steady. "But I think it means that we're supposed to do this every damn chance we get."

"Really?"

"Uh-huh."

"Oh, goody," he said. "You know how I feel about f—"

"Trevor!"

Her laughter followed him all the way into the bathroom.

9

As Lee stared at the bathroom door, her grin faded. She was in trouble. Big trouble.

Of all the possible outcomes of making love to Trevor, this was one she'd never considered. She'd imagined it terrible. Okay. Fun. Awkward. Interesting. But she hadn't imagined it would be the most powerful, earthshaking, intense experience of her life. And she had *never* imagined herself feeling this way afterward.

Trevor was her friend. That hadn't changed. He loved her the way friends do. He'd stop a bullet for her, he'd tell her if she had spinach in her teeth, but he wasn't going to declare his undying devotion and ask her to be his wife. She didn't want him to, for heaven's sake. At least she'd always thought she didn't want him to.

She got up and slipped her nightgown on, wishing he'd hurry so she could wash. She needed something to do that would ground her back in reality. Give her a proverbial slap in the face. All her nonsense thoughts would disappear in the light of day. They had to.

But what if they didn't?

It wouldn't be fair. The whole idea of sex with

Trevor was to uncomplicate her life. Not add new dimensions of angst and self-torture. More than that, much more than that, it wasn't supposed to put the basic relationship in danger.

"All yours."

She spun around at Trevor's voice. He walked toward her, naked and clean and smiling so warmly it took her breath away. The urge to touch him was so strong, her hand went out to him without her permission.

He took her hand, turned it over and kissed her palm. The resultant frisson spread through her whole body, giving her goose bumps, erect nipples and a wave of warmth between her legs. She glanced down to see that he'd been affected, too. With only that briefest of kisses, that simple touch of his lips to her palm, he began to harden.

"Still hungry?" he asked.

She'd forgotten about the food in her turmoil. The desire to eat had fled, replaced by a hunger to hold him close, to touch him everywhere, to feel that explosion of pleasure once more. But she couldn't. Not after the last time. Not after the feelings that had hit her like a one-two punch.

Trevor touched the small of her back and drew her to him. She tried to avoid his gaze, but he lifted her chin with his finger so she would have to look in his eyes. "You okay?"

She nodded.

"Really?"

She nodded again. "I'm just not sure I'm ready for another go-round."

He kissed her cheek, then her lips, then her nose. "We can wait," he said. "It won't be easy, but I can be patient."

She smiled, loving the feathery kisses on her eyelids, her forehead, then back to her lips. When his hand ran down her back, stroking her gently, pressing her against his hard flesh, she knew it was hopeless. She was a goner, a slave to her desire.

She flicked his lips with her tongue, and the debate ended. Trevor swept her up in his arms and carried her to the bed. He laid her down tenderly, then climbed in next to her.

She sighed, surrendering to the moment. She'd worry later.

TREVOR WOKE UP the next morning so hungry, it redefined the term. He could eat a horse. Hell, he could eat a whole herd. But he'd settle for waffles. Lots of them. With eggs. Maybe a couple of strips of bacon. Coffee. Juice. He moaned, but cut it short when he saw that Lee was still sleeping.

God, she looked beautiful. Her hair a glorious mess on the pillow, her eyelashes resting on her pale cheeks. He turned away, careful not to look at the rest of her. He didn't want to wake her, because if he did, he'd have to make love again, and frankly, he needed fuel. He'd been wrung out and left to dry, totally wasted, and he felt pretty damn proud. Four times. It had to be a record. At least for a guy his age.

He should call the Guinness people on Monday. At the very least, he should notify the *Post*.

Grinning, he slipped out of bed and gathered his clothes together. He managed to get to the bathroom and shut the door without looking at her even once.

He turned on the tub faucet, adjusted the temperature, then went to shave and brush his teeth. Jeez, he looked like hell. He didn't care. He felt too good to worry about a little thing like that.

Who would have thought? He squeezed a dollop of toothpaste on his brush and went at it vigorously, all the while staring at his face, wondering what he'd done to deserve all this.

Lee had been right. He'd been a fool to doubt her. It was the most perfect arrangement in the world. No fuss, no muss. Just plain fantastic sex with someone he was nuts about, without all the expectations, guilt, promises or disappointments. He could see the next few years in front of him, and he liked what he saw. No more singles' bars. No more blind dates. No more complications.

He had to hand it to her. Her idea had been inspired.

He finished brushing his teeth, rinsed, then got out his razor and shaving cream. One check on the tub told him he didn't have to rush, so he leisurely lathered up his stubble and took particular care shaving. Toward the end there, his five-o'clock shadow had turned into a next-morning beard, and he didn't want to scratch Lee when he kissed her.

Which he planned to do quite frequently.

The thought made him grin, and he nicked his chin. After a rousing curse, he finished the job, tacked a tiny piece of toilet paper on the cut, then turned to his bath.

The tub had filled nicely, with warm steam rising in whirls that fogged the mirror and windows. He stepped in, sighing as he lowered himself into the water.

Things couldn't have been more perfect. Except for perhaps breakfast on a tray, and Lee sitting opposite him.

He closed his eyes, and her image formed. Gasping for breath, shuddering with her climax. Then the picture changed and he saw her sleeping—calm, beautiful, vulnerable.

The memories of how he used to fantasize about her swirled around his head in concert with the steam. After they'd met, he'd done that a lot. Awake or asleep, Lee had filled his dreams. Even after he realized that they were going to be friends, and not lovers. Eventually, he'd banished the wicked thoughts. They were too dangerous, and too depressing. But every once in a while, he'd awaken hard, and he'd know she'd been there as he slept.

As exciting as his imagination had made those dream encounters, they all paled in comparison to the real deal. He'd never been more aroused. He hadn't known he could be that aroused. No other woman had ever affected him this way.

Maybe it was because he'd suppressed his desire for so long. Or maybe it was because of the arrangement they'd made. Who knows, maybe it was just because they fit. Comfortable, easy, with no strings attached. Whatever the reason, he didn't care. As long as she would have him, he'd be happy. Tired, but happy.

He sighed again, the sound itself relaxing his shoulders. For the first time in a long, long time, he felt utterly, completely content.

LEE PULLED her seat belt on and waited for Trevor to get in the car. It was time to go back, to leave this magic place, and all the little miracles that had occurred over the weekend. Real life loomed, only a few hours away. She didn't want to go.

It had been a perfect weekend. They hadn't gone out much. Mainly for meals, and once for a walk in the moonlight. Mostly, they'd made love. Oh, how they'd made love.

Trevor climbed in and shut his door, and the sound snapped her back to the problem at hand. What was she going to do now? The light of day had come twice, and it hadn't chased her worries away. If she'd thought she was in trouble on Friday night, it was nothing compared to Sunday afternoon.

Somehow, despite her best intentions, her heart had gotten involved. Trevor had been the most perfect lover she'd ever had. Not only was he inventive and passionate, but he'd been considerate, funny, intuitive. It had finally occurred to her this morning, just after he'd brought her coffee while she soaked in the tub, that he was the man of her dreams. He fit the checklist exactly. All the things she'd been looking for, but had never found.

It made sense. He was the best friend she'd ever had. Once she'd discovered he was such a compatible lover, the package was complete. Except for one tiny detail: the whole thing was completely out of the question.

She didn't want to love him *that way*. He didn't want to love her *that way*. All she'd wanted to do was add sex. So why in hell was she thinking about *romance*?

"You okay?"

She smiled and nodded at Trevor as he started the car.

"You sure? I've been watching. You look like something's wrong."

"You mean besides the fact that we're going back to the real world?"

He grinned, although she could only see his profile as he focused on pulling out of the driveway. She'd debated telling him about her quandary, but in the end, she'd decided not to. He didn't need to know she was this insane. That her rational mind had gone five seconds after he'd kissed her. When she got home, she'd talk to Katy about it.

"So what's up for you this week?"

"Not much." She had to think for a minute to remember her schedule. It felt like they'd been on the moon, not just to Connecticut. "I've got a couple of client lunches. And I promised Susan I'd go with her to get a dress for the wedding."

"Oh, man, I forgot about that. It's next Saturday, isn't it?"

She nodded. "Yep. Black tie."

"What about a present?"

"Don't worry. You're covered. We put Susan in charge, and she got everything. She'll give you a bill."

"Thank heaven for Susan."

"I'm just surprised she's going to this wedding at all," Lee said as she watched the beautiful scenery whoosh past. "She used to date David."

"When?"

"In college."

"No, she didn't."

Lee smiled. "Yes, she did."

"Where was I?"

"It was brief. Torrid. It didn't end well."

"That's not terribly surprising," he said. "Poor Susan. I wish she had someone."

"Not yet," Lee said. "It's too soon. She has to recover from Larry first."

Trevor looked at her, then back at the road. "You don't think it would be good for her to meet some nice guy?"

"Sure it would. But that's not who she'd meet. She'd end up with another Larrylike substance."

"How do you know?"

"Because that's her pattern. We all do that. Get involved with the same kind of person over and over, until we finally break the chain. I mean, look at you."

"What about me?"

"Every one of the women you've been semiserious about has been the same type."

"And what type is that?"

"Attractive in an icy kind of way. Intelligent. Selfish. Easily bored. And they all have a fatal flaw."

"Is that so?"

"Yes, that's so."

"What about you?"

"I'm not immune. I always pick guys who are emotionally unavailable. Who can't commit. At least they can't commit to me"

"Lucky you came up with this brilliant idea, eh?"

She turned to the window so he couldn't see her face. The second she'd said those words, she'd gotten it. What she'd done. How could she be so *stupid*? Of all the men in the whole world, there wasn't anyone more unavailable than Trevor. He absolutely, positively, would never get married. He'd told her that a hundred times, and proved it with every woman he'd been with.

It was ridiculous to think they could.... It didn't even bear repeating. She'd been a romantic fool, but she felt better now. Clearer. Of course she didn't love Trevor. Not *love* love. It had been that room. The fire. The novelty.

"Where are you?"

She turned back to face him. "I'm here," she said. "Very much here."

"I'm glad," he said. "You know, I almost backed out of this."

"Really?"

He nodded. "Up until the last minute, I wasn't sure I wanted to go through with it." He found her hand and squeezed it. "But I'm damn glad I did."

"Are you?"

He gave her a puzzled look. "Of course. Aren't you?"

"Sure, sure. It was a fantastic weekend. I'm just thinking...."

"That's dangerous."

"About how it's going to work back in the city."

"Ah," he said. "I have some ideas about that."

"Do tell."

"Okay," he said. "First, I think we need to have the ground rules in place."

"Oh?"

"Yeah. For instance, spending the night is optional."

"Uh-huh."

"We don't have to do it every time we see each other. Although, I can't imagine not wanting to."

"Thank you."

"And if anything gets wiggy, we talk about it. Right away."

"Wiggy?"

"Yeah. Uncomfortable. Say, you meet Mr. Right tomorrow. You tell me tomorrow night."

"Or if you meet the woman of your dreams?"

"I have," he said, smiling happily. "You're everything I've ever wanted. Beautiful. Funny. Great in the sack. And you don't want to live together, or God forbid, get married. What else could a man ask for?"

"Right," she agreed, even though her chest constricted until she could barely catch her breath. "Absolutely right."

TREVOR PULLED UP in front of Lee's building, and turned off the car. He hated to wake her. She looked so peaceful, resting her head on his jacket, propped up against the window. Poor kid. She was exhausted. Not surprising since they'd had so much exercise and so little sleep. And yet, he wasn't ready for it to end. He wanted her.

This was highly unusual. There had been other weekends with other women, and they had all ended with him so anxious to get home that he had to work at being pleasant.

Not this time. It was just so damn comfortable with Lee. He didn't have to ask about her family, and she certainly knew about his. All the chitchat that comes with getting to know someone had already been dispensed with, so they were free to talk about the good stuff. Or not talk at all.

Maybe this is what it was like for Katy and Ben. Not having much experience with happy couples, Trevor couldn't be sure. His parents changed spouses like some people traded in cars. Two years seemed to be the magic number, although his mother had been with what's-his-name for three and a half. A record. But that had ended, too. Just like all the others.

He'd stopped going to the weddings after a while. It had seemed so pointless. What he couldn't figure out was why they got married at all. It would be so much cleaner if they just lived together. But each time, his mother swore it was the last time. That she'd finally found true love. His father wasn't that sentimental. As he got older, the wives kept getting younger. Eventually, Trevor supposed, he'd be marrying a fetus.

Not once, not even when his parents had been married to each other, had he felt they had the kind of comfortable, easy relationship he had with Lee. It occurred to him that neither of his parents had liked their mates very much.

He felt lucky to have found Lee. And glad that he'd taken the time to get to know her as well as he had. That they'd become friends. And damn glad they'd become lovers.

"Are we home?"

"Yeah. Just got here."

Lee sat up, blinked the sleep away and patted her hair down. "I'm sorry. I didn't know I was going to do that."

"No sweat," he said, unbuckling his seat belt. "I'm glad you got some rest."

"You must be exhausted."

"No, actually. I feel pretty good."

She undid her own seat belt and got out of the car. He watched her stretch, lifting her arms high in the air, which raised her sweater so that he caught a glimpse of her tummy. The leggings she wore fit her body snugly enough for him to see all her curves. He wanted her.

She headed for the trunk and he hurried out, wondering if it would be too pushy to ask to stay the night. Or maybe he should just go upstairs and see what happened.

He pressed the electronic key and the trunk popped up. He reached for her bags, but she beat him to it. "You don't have to come up," she said. "I can manage."

The disappointment surprised him. Not that he felt it, but that it was so acute. "I don't mind," he said. "It's no problem."

"Suit yourself."

He took the bigger of the two bags and followed Lee inside her building. The doorman smiled at her—or maybe leered was a better word for it. Trevor hadn't noticed this guy before. He was a lot younger than the other one. Trevor hated him on sight.

Lee led him to the elevator, oblivious to his reaction. They rode up quietly, her leaning against the wall, eyes closed. They got to her floor, and he followed her to her apartment, watching how she leaned a bit to her left with the weight of the suitcase. How her hair swayed across her back.

When she got to her door, she fished out her keys and went inside. He followed, knowing he shouldn't be hoping she'd ask him to stay, but hoping anyway.

The cats were there to greet her, and she picked up both of them to carry them to the couch. He closed the door, debating whether he should say something. Maybe she assumed he didn't want to stay, and that's why she didn't ask.

"I missed you," she said to Ira, while scratching George behind the ear. "Were you good boys?"

They answered her with purrs, and with a great deal of face rubbing. Trevor knew just how they felt.

Lee looked at him and smiled. She put the cats on the couch, and stood up again. With each step she took toward him, his hope diminished. He could see it in her eyes. She wanted him to go.

Which was fine. No problem. It was silly to have thought otherwise. The weekend was over.

"Thank you," she said, taking his hands in hers. "It was the best weekend I've ever had."

"Me, too."

"I imagine we'll both get lots of phone calls tonight."

He laughed. "What do you say we torture them, and don't answer?"

She shook her head. "They'd never give up. Or forgive us."

"Yeah," he said, wanting to kiss her. Wanting to do a lot more than kiss her.

She stood on tiptoe, and gave him a quick peck on the cheek. "I love you," she said.

He smiled. "I love you, too."

"Now go get some sleep. It's back to the salt mines in the morning."

"Right," he said.

"You okay?"

"Sure. I'm fine." He stepped back and reached for the doorknob. "I'll call you tomorrow."

"Great."

"Bye."

She waved her fingers at him. Waited for him to get the hell out. So he did.

The whole way back to the car, he wondered what it meant, if he'd gotten things wrong. But then he thought about last night. How she'd looked at him when they made love.

They might be back in the real world, but it wasn't the same world. Things would never be the same again.

He whistled as he got into the car.

10

"WELL?"

"If you don't start talking soon, there's going to be bloodshed."

Lee looked at Katy and Susan, sitting across the table from her at Veselka, her favorite little Ukrainian restaurant. The pirogi had just been brought to the table, with lovely sides of crisp sautéed onions and beet relish. She'd been dreaming of pirogi for the past month, wanting them desperately, but now that they were here, she seemed to have lost her appetite.

"It was nice," she said, keeping her voice down so that the other diners in the small café couldn't hear, even though the Monday night crowd was pretty light.

"Nice?" Susan gave her a look that singed her eyelashes. "*Nice?* That's all you're going to say?"

Lee was just as surprised as her friends at her reluctance to talk about the weekend. Since college, they'd shared everything: the good, the bad and the ugly. So, why wasn't she telling them about Trevor? These were her best buddies. Surely they could help with her confusion, and her doubt. They knew Trevor almost as well as she did, so their insights would be particularly useful.

Dammit, everything was going haywire. It wasn't enough that she was feeling all mushy over Trevor, but now she couldn't even talk to Katy and Susan.

"What happened?" Katy asked again.

Susan shook her head. "Couldn't he get it up?"

Lee coughed, glad she hadn't been eating anything. She'd have choked.

"If she doesn't want to tell us, then she doesn't have to," Katy said, but it was just a line. Lee could tell she was dying for details. And why shouldn't she tell them? Maybe if she did, she'd stop blowing things out of proportion.

"Okay," she said. "It was fantastic. More than fantastic. It was the single best experience of my life. Are you happy now?"

Katy looked at Susan, then back at Lee. "So, you're upset because...?"

"Because it was the single best experience of my life."

"Ah." Susan nodded. "Now I get it." Then she turned to Katy and rolled her eyes.

"I'm not complaining," Lee said. "Honest. It was better than my wildest dreams. But..."

Susan, her hair pulled back in a ponytail, her outfit an Audrey Hepburn ensemble, complete with black turtleneck, black capris and little black ballet slippers, stuck her fork into a steaming potato dumpling and proceeded to put the whole thing in her mouth.

Katy ignored Susan and touched Lee's hand. "Come on. Maybe we can help."

"You can't. No one can. I've made this bed, and, pardon the pun, but I have to sleep in it."

Susan lifted her hand for silence, swallowed twice, then said, "What bed? What the hell happened?"

"I just didn't count on it being so...so..."

"What, for God's sake?" Katy said, her voice just this side of desperate.

"So romantic."

Katy and Susan exchanged glances again. Then they looked at her as if she'd gone neatly around the bend.

"Don't you get it?" she said. "It was supposed to be sex. Plain, simple, don't-let-the-door-slam-you-on-the-ass sex."

"And it turned out to be what?" Susan asked.

Lee sighed, sat back in her chair, shook her head. "The goddamn earth moved. The angels wept. There was a great hue and cry across the land."

"Wow," Katy said. "We are talking about you and Trevor, right?"

"Of course. Dammit, I wasn't supposed to *feel* anything."

"Honey," Susan said, "if that was your expectation, I think you've been doing it wrong."

"I meant emotionally. Romantically."

"Oh," Katy said, stretching the word into a little song. "That's not good."

"No kidding." Lee couldn't stand it. She took a pirogi and cut it on her plate, added some onions and beets and ate it. It was beyond heavenly, and she took three more dumplings from the big platter.

"I still don't see what the problem is," Susan said. "You love him, he loves you. It was great between the sheets. You should be happy."

"I should be a size two, but I'm not. Susan, I don't want to be in love with Trevor. I don't want to want Trevor. Get it?"

"Maybe he feels the same way. Maybe it's not a problem."

Katy shook her head. "Trevor doesn't want a relationship."

Lee nodded. "That's an understatement. I don't either, not really. I mean, if I'd wanted a relationship, I wouldn't have done it with him. He was supposed to be my safe guy."

Katy, still dressed in her attorney clothes, a gray tweed suit with a pale-blue silk blouse, tucked her napkin under her chin and dug in to the pirogi. It should have looked ridiculous, but it didn't. In a weird way, the napkin bib was charming. "So," she said between bites. "What now? Does he know?"

"No, he doesn't. I'm not going to tell him, either."

"Are you going to sleep with him again?" Susan asked.

"No. Well, maybe. Oh, God, I hope so."

Katy laughed. "I still can't get over it. Trevor made the angels weep. How do you like that."

"I like it too much. Oh, man, he did everything right. More than right. It was like out of a movie. The room, the fire, the champagne."

Susan's right brow lifted. "You had champagne?"

Lee nodded. "And you should have seen this bathroom. A claw-foot tub for two."

"Don't tell me," Katy said. "You did a *Bull Durham*, right?"

Susan's left brow lifted so she had a matched pair. "Huh?"

"*Bull Durham*," Lee explained. "Susan Sarandon and Kevin Costner. They took a bath together."

"Not *a* bath," Katy said. "*The* bath. Candles everywhere, sloshing water. Susan, you have to see the movie. I've told you that before."

"Baseball isn't my thing."

"Baseball isn't what the movie's about," Katy said. "Personally, I give it four vibrators. My highest rating."

Lee laughed.

"Remember that scene in *The Big Easy*? This one is better."

Susan shrugged her shoulders. "Okay, I'll watch it this weekend." She sipped her tea for a moment. "Four vibrators, huh?"

Katy grinned. "Have a change of batteries on hand." She turned to Lee. "What's the plan, kiddo?"

"I don't have one. I'm so afraid of making him uncomfortable. I don't want to risk the friendship."

"Your feelings are that strong?"

Lee nodded. "That strong plus ten. I don't know what to do."

"Give yourself a little time," Susan said. "Don't see him for a while. Give it a chance to blow over."

"Good idea," Lee said. "I just won't see him.

That's all. At least for a week, maybe two. By then, I'm sure I'll be able to think more clearly."

TREVOR PICKED UP the phone on the second ring and carried it with him to the bedroom. "Hello."

"Hey."

It was Ben, so Trevor went on changing clothes.

"How was your weekend?"

"Great."

"Good. That's great."

"Yeah," Trevor said, making sure the T-shirt he'd picked was clean and had no stains.

"So, you think this thing is gonna happen?" Ben asked.

"Yeah. I'm heading over to her place now."

"I thought she was out to dinner with the girls."

"Hold on a sec." Trevor put the phone on the bed as he slipped the T-shirt on, then picked it up again. "They just finished. Lee called from the restaurant."

"Okay. Great. See you on Saturday."

"Huh?"

"The wedding."

Trevor nodded. "Oh, yeah. Okay. See you then." He hung up, then headed to the bathroom to shave. Maybe he should leave a razor over at Lee's. Nah. She'd probably think he meant something by it, and be put off. The last thing he wanted to do was scare her.

TREVOR SLIPPED Lee his handkerchief. She sniffed, then dabbed under her eyes. When he looked over at

Katy, sitting on his other side, he saw she was crying, too. What was it about women and weddings?

He leaned back, and saw Ben staring at the ceiling. Trevor couldn't see Susan, but Peter, who sat on the aisle, wasn't watching the happy couple, either. Peter was staring at something across the way, and when Trevor tried to figure out what, he saw Andy Broeder, another college friend. Interesting. Peter and Andy had been an item for about ten minutes during senior year, but then Peter had discovered theater arts, and that was the end of that.

Sighing, Trevor turned his attention back to the ceremony. The rabbi was speaking Hebrew to David and Marilyn, which he knew for a fact the groom didn't understand. David had confessed years ago that he'd only learned enough of the traditional language to get through his bar mitzvah, then promptly forgotten everything. Maybe Marilyn understood. Or maybe the ritual was so ingrained that no one had to understand each word. The gist was clear: love, honor, cherish. Sickness and health. Yada, yada, yada. What the rabbi should be asking is if these two people had the same spending habits. Were they both night people, or early risers? Did they have a sense of humor, and would he promise, on pain of death, to put his clothes into the hamper instead of on the floor?

But they never talked about that stuff at weddings. They went for the mystical, which was well and good, but it didn't do squat to insure a compatible marriage. There ought to be a test, a real test, that had questions about toilet seats and toothpaste caps. His parents would have failed that one. Each time. Which would have been better for everyone.

Ben and Katy? They'd pass that test. And now that he had almost a whole week under his belt, so to speak, with Lee, he knew they would pass it, too. Not that they were heading in that direction, but the compatibility test was also useful for other relationships. Friends who slept with friends, for example. God, it sounded like a Jerry Springer show.

He looked down, and saw a couple of stray gray hairs on his tuxedo pants. George. Or Ira. The cats had welcomed him with a leg rub when he'd picked Lee up for this soiree. Man, had she looked gorgeous.

His gaze slid next door, looking first at her face, still a little teary-eyed and wistful. Then he perused the dress. It was a new one, he thought. He'd have remembered it if he'd seen if before. Hunter-green, off the shoulder, it reminded him of something Kim Bassinger would have worn in *L.A. Confidential*. The long slim skirt and the tailored waist made Lee look delicious, and her hair, all wavy like that, made him think of Rita Hayworth.

He liked her in the dress, but he liked her better out of it. As he thought the words, she turned and smiled at him for just a second, then went back to watching the action under the *chupa*. He kept his focus on her. On the most amazing week he'd ever had.

His days had been excellent. He'd felt sharper

than a blade, completely on his game. His articles had been easy to write. His editor had asked him to work on a major wine guide. He'd even managed to take down all the dark wood paneling in his den. Of course now he had to figure out what to do with the walls, but that wasn't the issue. The thing was, he felt able to take on the world.

Because of one woman.

She sniffed again, and he watched her cry. Her eyelashes had become wet and spiky, and he had the sudden urge to kiss the moisture away. What was she doing to him?

Whatever it was, he hoped it wouldn't stop anytime soon. Their nights together had been indescribable. Every time he felt they'd reached the pinnacle, they went higher, hotter, deeper. All she had to do was look at him, and he sprang to attention like a private on parade. He couldn't get enough of her.

The rabbi was speaking English again, and it sounded like he was heading toward home plate. David said his vows, and Marilyn said hers. The ring went on her finger. Then David smashed the glass under his foot, and a chorus of *"Mazel Tovs"* filled the sanctuary.

Lee grabbed Trevor's hand, and she squeezed it tight. For a wild second, just as David and Marilyn kissed for the first time as husband and wife, Trevor saw himself as Lee's groom. He saw himself growing old with her by his side. As if looking through a kaleidoscope, he saw a completely different kind of life than he'd ever imagined before. Little pictures, tumbling one on top of the other, of laughter, making love, feeding babies and waking up each day to her smile.

It ended as quickly as it had hit. Once more, he was just a guy in the fifth row of the temple, standing up to watch as the new couple walked down the aisle. But he didn't breathe well for a while. Not until he realized that it was the atmosphere, the wedding and all those crying women that had gotten to him. No big deal. Just one of those moments that had no relevance at all.

LEE SAT DOWN between Susan and Trevor. She'd repaired her face, wiping away all traces of her sentimental tears. Katy and Ben sat across from her, and Peter's seat was there, too, only she hadn't seen him since they'd walked from the sanctuary to the banquet room.

Everything looked so beautiful. The bride's colors were powder-blue and white, and the decorations followed that scheme down to the napkins and matchbooks. The floral centerpieces mixed blue irises and orchids: simple, elegant and as chic as the bride herself.

"God, I hate weddings."

Lee turned sharply to shush Susan. Everyone else had the same idea and it ended up sounding like the table had sprung a leak.

"Well, I *do*. It's a horrible custom. You know where it came from? Property. Ownership. Men invented marriage so that they would have a line of descendants. It had nothing to do with love. And back then, people only lived to, like, thirty or something, and when they got married for life, they were looking at fifteen years, tops. They'd have laughed themselves silly if they heard people were supposed to be a couple for fifty years."

"Susan," Katy said, "your point is well taken, and your logic impeccable. But if you don't keep your voice down, I'm going to throttle you."

"Fine," Susan said, grabbing her glass of kosher Chablis. "I won't say another word."

"Didn't she look incredible?" Katy said to no one in particular. "I never used to think Marilyn was that... She's just bloomed, don't you think? David's crazy about her. They're gonna try for kids right away."

Lee had reached for her water glass, but she paused. Something was funny about Katy's voice. She couldn't put her finger on it, but it wasn't normal somehow.

Katy looked at Ben, then he whispered something to her, looked around the room, and got up. He took off, leaving a smiling Katy behind.

"What's going on?" Lee asked, looking at Trevor to see if he knew something. But he wasn't even paying attention. The band had started playing, and Trevor seemed fascinated by the violinist.

She turned back to Katy, but before she could ask what was up, Ben came back to the table, Peter in tow. The boys sat down and Peter grabbed his wine. Ben grabbed Katy's hand and nodded, and Katy kissed him lightly on the lips before facing the group. "We have an announcement."

Lee's pulse kicked into high gear, and her tummy clenched. It could only be one thing. The one thing the two of them wanted more than anything else, that they'd been praying for for over a year.

"We're pregnant," Katy said, her joy making her voice go high, making her smile shine like sunlight.

The roar from their table caused a minor ruckus, but Lee didn't care one bit. This was the happiest news in the world. No child could be luckier. No parents would be better. The tears Lee had so carefully patted dry came back with a vengeance. She jumped to her feet, and scrambled to hug her friends, bumping into Trevor and Susan and Peter. They were all laughing and crying, hugging and squeezing. Then she found herself in Trevor's arms. Her gaze met his, and the room around her faded to a blur. There was only Trevor. And a future so clear she could almost touch it. A future she could never have.

He bent to kiss her, but she moved, breaking out of his embrace. "Excuse me," she mumbled.

She heard him call after her as she hurried to the rest room. The band played Gershwin. "Someone to Watch Over Me." Couples danced, cheek to cheek. The waiters filed in, carrying big silver trays.

Lee made it through the door, but stopped short as she saw the bride standing just outside the ballroom, preparing to toss her bouquet. A dozen single women shuffled and joked and tried to hide the fact that they were all willing her to throw it to them. Lee couldn't watch. She walked faster, trying to pass the women without calling attention to herself.

The bouquet hit her on the back of the head.

11

TREVOR KISSED KATY, hugging her tight. He felt really happy for her, and for Ben. It felt odd, though. A kid. It would change things, and not only for the parents. Their little gang wouldn't be the same, not ever again. For that, he felt sad. But nothing stays the same forever. People grow up. Or at least grow older.

"Where did Lee go?"

He shook his head. "I think to the bathroom."

Katy's brows came down in concern. "Is she okay?"

"As far as I know."

She took his hands from around her waist. "Go after her, okay?"

He smiled. "You're gonna be the best damn mother in the history of motherhood."

"I don't know about that, but the baby will never lack for love and attention. Isn't that right, Uncle Trevor?"

"Damn straight."

"Now, go find her."

He pushed his chair in, listening to Peter's excitement as he talked about having "their" baby. The guy was practically bouncing off the walls.

Ben looked like the cat who ate the canary. Smug didn't do him justice. He'd finally hit that home run.

The only one who wasn't flying high as a kite was Susan. She stood a little behind Peter, her hands gripping her wineglass, looking as cool and beautiful as a princess. She smiled, but it wasn't real. There was too much sadness in her eyes to make it work. Poor kid. She was probably thinking about the kids she could have had if Larry hadn't been the schmuck of the century.

Trevor went over to her and kissed her just below her right ear. She jumped, but then she laughed, and it was good to hear that. "You okay?" he asked quietly.

"Of course. I'm thrilled for them. What could be better?"

He nodded, then kissed her on the cheek. "Your time will come," he whispered. "The man who catches you will be the luckiest son of a bitch in New York."

"Thanks," she said. Then she went for her purse and started looking through it as if she'd lost something important. He left, not wanting to embarrass her by seeing her cry.

He made his way past linen-covered tables, tuxedoed waiters, and a gaggle of giggling women. Outside the ballroom door, he found the bride and groom kissing at the bottom of the staircase. It wasn't the same kind of kiss as the one under the canopy. This one was more about the honeymoon than the wedding.

As Trevor headed toward the rest room, it occurred to him that he'd go back to the bed-and-breakfast for his honeymoon. He stopped dead. *His honeymoon?* What, was he crazy? Was it something in the water?

"What's wrong?" Lee stood in front of the ladies' room door. She looked at him funny, as if she'd known what he was thinking, and found it as weird as he did.

"I'm fine. What about you?"

"I'm fine."

"Good," he said, wondering if the uneasiness in his chest was caused by his foolish thoughts, or if something was really bothering Lee. He tried hard to be perceptive and to read between the lines, but he never got it right. Not with women, at least.

"So, we'd better get back," Lee said, sounding just as uncomfortable as he felt. "Unless you have to..." She glanced at the men's room door.

"No, no. We can go."

"Okay."

Neither of them moved. Or blinked. They just stood staring at each other with unasked questions floating between them. Trevor couldn't stand it. He shifted his gaze first. "That's great about Katy, huh?"

"Yeah, it is," Lee said, and if he wasn't mistaken, there was relief in her reply. "They're going to be great parents."

"I'll say."

Lee started walking back to the ballroom, and he moved in beside her. Knowing he was taking a risk, he squared his shoulders and decided to jump. "Are you sad because you want kids?"

She stopped so fast he had to turn around and backtrack. He couldn't tell if the shocked expression on her face was because his speculation was so outrageous it defied logic, or if he'd hit the nail on the head.

"Sad?" she said, but more to herself than him.

He nodded. "I guess a woman your age has that old biological clock ticking away."

The left corner of her mouth quirked up in a cockeyed grin. "Women my age, huh?"

His stomach sank. He'd been way off base. "I didn't mean—"

She waved her hand dismissively. "It's okay. You're not in trouble."

"Thank God for small favors," he said, vowing to keep his big, fat mouth shut from now on.

She ignored his smart-ass comment. "I think you're right. I think I am a little sad."

"Well, sure." His chest swelled as he congratulated himself on being right, for once. "It's only natural. I mean, you're almost thirty, with no prospect of a husband in sight—"

"Quit while you're ahead, Trevor."

"Oh."

She shook her head at him, then grabbed his hand and led him back toward the ballroom.

"Lee?"

She put her finger up to her lips and said, "Shh."

He thought about it, and decided she was right.

Discretion being the better part of valor, and all that. Besides, he had no business trying to guess what Lee was thinking. She confused him now more than ever. She made him think crazy thoughts, and feel things he had no business feeling.

The only thing he was completely certain about was that he wanted her. Once they were in bed, all the confusion disappeared like magic.

She opened the door to the banquet room, and he heard the band play "Makin' Whoopee." "Amen to that," he whispered. Whoopee was fun. Whoopee, he could handle. It was making love that turned him into an utter fool.

SHE SHOULDN'T have asked him back to her apartment. But then maybe she was a born masochist, taking some sick pleasure in torturing herself. It was as if she were dying of thirst and a big, frosty glass of water was just out of reach. She could have Trevor, but she couldn't *have* Trevor.

One thing was certain. She had to get over this romantic fantasy of the two of them walking hand in hand into the sunset, or she had to stop sleeping with him. That first option didn't look so good. For whatever reason, her twisted little brain had gone into hyperdrive starting that first night, and it refused to let the notion alone. Despite her best intentions, she couldn't shake the idea of marriage. Just last week she'd found herself doodling on a scratch pad: Mrs. Trevor Templeton. Mrs. Lee Templeton. Lee Templeton. Lee Phillips-Templeton.

It was insane.

She understood that biology played a part in her craziness. Women need to pair-bond as an instinctive survival tool for their future children. She knew that making love, for a woman, was more emotional than physical. That her feelings for Trevor reflected some deep primal response that had more to do with procreation then recreation. But knowing all that didn't mean squat. Logic had nothing to do with it. She needed him on a cellular level, a need that overpowered any cognitive functions.

He just thought she was a fun romp in the hay.

She wanted a happily-ever-after that she could never have.

And yet, here she was, in her bathroom, toothbrush in hand, minutes away from climbing into bed with him, her body already priming itself with tightened nipples, dilated pupils and an ache that wouldn't ease.

What she should do was put down the toothbrush, march to the bedroom, and tell him, point-blank, that it wasn't working. That he was wonderful, it had nothing to do with him, it was all her, but that they couldn't do it again. Not even once.

He'd be baffled, and he'd be upset; at least, she assumed he would be. He might even be hurt. But in the long run, it was the wisest course of action. In a few weeks, maybe a month or two, she'd tell him why. Once she was over him, it wouldn't be too embarrassing to explain that she'd gone a little nuts. He'd understand. He would.

She put her toothbrush down, then picked it up again. No reason to have bad breath when she delivered the bad news, right? As she scrubbed her molars, she rehearsed her speech. *Trevor*, she'd begin. *This has been the most wonderful week of my life, and I owe it all to you. But I don't think it would be a good idea to continue. It's not you. It's me.*

Good. Short. To the point. No emotional outpouring and no tears.

She rinsed, got the Scope and gargled, then ran a quick brush through her hair. It was time. She was strong. Flinging open the door, she walked out, shoulders back, head held high, determination filling her with courage.

He was already under the covers. Naked. His perfect chest bared to the waist. He threw back the covers for her to join him, as he gave her a slow, sensuous smile.

She could do this.

He patted the bed, and she sat down, turning so she'd face him. She opened her mouth, and promptly forgot her speech. She didn't panic, though. She could wing it. "Trevor," she said, searching frantically for the next word.

He sat up, scooted down until he was right next to her. Then he kissed her. Right below her ear, in that secret little hollow spot. Goose bumps sprang up all over her body, and when he nibbled her earlobe, she moaned helplessly.

"What is it?" he whispered, then he went back to teasing her with his teeth.

"Trevor," she said again, only this time it came out all breathy, like Marilyn Monroe on Prozac.

"Yes?" he said, forming the word while his lips rested on her neck so she felt the vibration and the heat from his mouth.

"Nothing," she said, then she turned, threw her arms around his neck and kissed him so hard they both fell backward.

He lifted her nightshirt, and ran his hand up her thigh. All coherence ended the second he hit pay dirt. Distantly, as if from another room, or another planet, she remembered that she was supposed to tell him something. But that could wait. Especially when his fingers moved inside her.

She moaned as he thrust his two fingers deep, then withdrew, only to thrust again, harder this time. Deeper.

He didn't release her from his kiss. He kept increasing the pressure, in and out, harder and deeper, until she had to throw her leg over his hip so he could bring her to the brink.

Just as she started up the steep hill toward climax, he stopped. He got to his knees and scooped her up, lifting her completely off the bed. He kissed her once more, then smiled a very wicked smile.

The next thing she knew, she was on the bed again, only this time, she lay on her stomach. Trevor swung his leg over her thighs, and lifted her from the waist until she was on her knees.

He moved his body over hers, running his hands over her breasts and her stomach, then back to her breasts, taking special care with her nipples, squeezing softly, flicking the tips with his thumbs.

She buried her head in the pillow, and then he moved again. She felt those wicked thumbs at her nether lips, opening her to his gaze. His moan wafted over the bed as he thrust himself inside her, making her forget about fingers and teasing. Making her forget everything. He went in fast and hard, all the way to the hilt, his body slapping against hers.

She gasped as he withdrew almost all the way, hesitated one agonizing second, then plunged in again.

Over and over, he entered her. Just when she thought it couldn't get any better, he leaned down and, while his left hand held her steady, his right hand slipped down past her stomach, tugged gently on her pubic hair, then found her swollen bud. Like a magician, he rubbed her flesh until her whole body tensed, seconds away from the edge of madness.

Then he thrust once more, crying out as he came, making her come on the same wave. Time stopped as she shuddered to her climax, as they climaxed together.

Much later, Trevor fell asleep with his head on her pillow. She lay awake for a long time, watching him. She didn't even realize she was weeping until she felt the moisture on the pillow.

TREVOR CONTEMPLATED his menu, which was ridiculous because he'd been to the Broadway Diner so often he knew it by heart. But today he couldn't decide. The others had ordered already, and the wait-ress tapped her pencil impatiently on her thumbnail. "Scrambled eggs, bacon, English muffin," he said, closing the menu just seconds before the waitress whipped it away.

"So, you guys meet here every week?"

It was Andy, Peter's friend from the wedding. In the three weeks since they'd gotten reacquainted, they'd certainly seemed to click, which Trevor thought was interesting. Andy wasn't Peter's usual type. Mostly, Peter chose actors or models with chis-eled features and limited vocabularies. The affairs ran their course in a matter of weeks, with Peter al-ways swearing it was the last time.

Andy wasn't an actor or a model. He was a com-puter programmer, of all things. Trevor didn't think Peter even had a computer. Andy wasn't chiseled, ei-ther. He was tall and lanky, with longish hair, and his nose was on the big side. But he seemed nice, and Peter looked smitten.

"Every Sunday," Katy answered. "For years, now."

"That's great," Andy said. "It keeps the friend-ships tight."

"That it does," Susan said, signaling the waitress for fresh coffee. "Anyone have any aspirin? Or mor-phine?"

Trevor shook his head. Poor Susan. She'd been drinking again. Since she'd heard the news about Katy's kid, she'd gotten smashed a lot. Four times that he knew of, in the past few weeks. She didn't look her usual cool self. Her eyes were puffy and her normally perfect hair was shoved under a baseball cap that said, Bad Hair Day.

But maybe it wasn't the aftereffects of alcohol that had Susan looking like death warmed over. Maybe Susan had the same bug Lee had picked up. She'd skipped their morning run, claiming an upset stomach. He looked at her, sitting next to him, at the moment deep in conversation with Katy. The topic was the baby, of course.

Lee didn't look her usual self, either. Her skin seemed pale, and her hands a bit shaky. They'd planned a trip to the flea market this afternoon, but he doubted they'd make it. After breakfast, he would put her back in bed. Only this time, he wouldn't join her. Which was the truest act of friendship he could think of.

He wanted her all the time. In restaurants, in book stores. Talking on the phone. Even while he wrote. She was like his own low-grade fever. He went on about his business, but the thought of her was always there. The feel of her skin always remembered.

He reached under the table, and found her hand. It was better when he touched her. She squeezed his hand, and he felt his shoulders relax.

Leaning over, close enough to smell the hint of vanilla behind her ear, he whispered, "You okay?"

She nodded. "Right as rain."

"Still, I think we ought to skip the flea market."

"Let's wait and see how we feel after breakfast."

As if Lee's words had conjured her, the waitress

chose that moment to come to the table with her heavy tray. Breakfast was served, and coffee freshened. The conversation was easy, with Andy fitting right in. Only Susan was quieter than normal, but even she perked up after she'd eaten a bit.

But Lee didn't eat even half her eggs and toast. No flea market for them. All he wanted to do was get her back home and in bed. To bring her juice, and to put his hand on her forehead to gauge her temperature. With an odd anticipation, he finished his meal, feeling foolish for looking forward to playing nursemaid.

"TREVOR, GO HOME." Lee made sure she sounded firm, insistent. That no part of her worry showed. He'd been mothering her for three hours now, putting her to bed, bringing her juice, and all the best parts of the Sunday paper, even though she'd told him she felt fine, that she had no temperature. He hadn't believed her, first feeling her forehead, then using a thermometer. But even he couldn't deny the 98.6 when he saw it.

"I don't know," he said. "Your color still isn't right."

"That's because I'm not wearing any makeup. If I put some on, will you leave?"

He smiled. "If I didn't know better, I'd swear you were trying to get rid of me."

"I am! Go home! Scoot." She gave him a gentle nudge with her foot, pushing at his leg. He didn't move from his position at the side of her bed. He just kept looking at her as if he had a special secret.

"I'm wounded to the core," he said, exaggerating a hurt tone.

"You are not. What you are is late with a deadline. I won't be held responsible when your editor gives you hell."

"I can work here."

"No, you can't. Besides, I have things to do."

"Oh, yeah? Like what?"

"Like get ready for the week. Like iron. Cook my chicken breasts and broccoli."

"I could do that," he said, albeit a little tentatively.

She laughed. "Yeah, right. When's the last time you ironed, big boy?"

"I beg your pardon," he said, crossing his arms over his chest. "I've ironed plenty."

"Really?"

He dropped his arms. "No. I've never ironed. I don't even own an iron."

"So, go the hell home. You've taken care of me brilliantly, but whatever I had this morning is completely gone. Now, all you're doing is bothering me."

His head crooked to the side, and his eyebrows came down in concern. "Really?"

"No," she said, unable to even tease that way. "But I'll feel better knowing you're getting your work done. Honest."

He leaned over and kissed her, first on her cheek, then her nose, and finally, on her lips. The last kiss lingered, reminding her that she was lying. That she wanted him to stay, not just this afternoon, but forever.

She had to break the kiss. And with it, a little piece of her heart. It wasn't a new feeling, or a new argument. She'd almost grown used to it in the past three weeks. Every time he walked out her door, she felt another piece crumble. Eventually, she supposed, there'd be nothing left. At least that would solve her problem. With no heart, there would be no pain.

Trevor stood up and grabbed the carafe on her nightstand. He walked out of the room, and while he was gone, she cursed the unfairness of it all. This afternoon, Trevor had shown himself to be incredibly caring. No man had ever nursed her, not even once. On the contrary. The few times she'd gotten sick while she was dating, her "boyfriends" had left so fast, they left skid marks. She'd never minded too much. She just figured that was the way things were.

Trevor had changed all that. Now she saw that the other men were more concerned about themselves than with the state of her health. Despite the sobriquet, not one of her former lovers had ever loved her. Or even cared enough to risk sharing a cold.

Not Trevor. Mindless of the germs, if there were any, he'd been attentive, solicitous, funny and so sweet it made her want to cry. But instead of feeling grateful, she felt cranky as hell. If he'd been a louse, or even if he'd been distracted, it would have made things much easier for her. She could have used his attitude to build a case against him, and in time, she would have gotten over this infatuation. But he hadn't given her one smidgen of ammunition.

For a man who didn't want a committed relationship, who swore that he was allergic to marriage and all marriage stood for, he was doing a pretty convincing husband act. Everything he did showed her his tenderness, his concern. If she hadn't known better, she'd have sworn he'd conquered his fear of commitment. And there, as they say, was the rub.

She had to get him out of here. Now. Before things got even more out of control. Before he touched her again, or God forbid, kissed her. She was inches away from confessing everything, from sharing her suspicions with him, and that would be a disaster.

He'd be appalled, maybe even feel betrayed. She'd have no defense—she was the one who'd set up the ground rules. Whatever his reaction, he'd distance himself so quickly, he'd probably break the land speed record. She wouldn't blame him. Especially if what she suspected was true.

He came back, the carafe filled with fresh orange juice. His smile warmed her more than the blanket he'd tucked under her chin. He put the juice down, hesitated as if he wanted to tell her something, but just nodded instead. "I'm off," he said, "although I'm not happy about it."

She smiled, afraid that if she spoke, the trembling she felt inside would affect her voice.

"You'll call me if you get worse?"

She nodded.

"Swear?"

She crossed her heart with her index finger.

"Okay. I'll call you later." Then he leaned down and kissed her again. Twice.

The second he turned to go to the door, she wiped her eyes, damning her traitorous tears. When he looked back a final time, there was no sign that she was anything but content. But as she heard him walk through the living room, heard the door open, then close, she sagged with the weight of her pretense.

It hadn't hit her until she'd talked with Katy. Until Katy had given her the details.

Lee couldn't be absolutely sure, not without a test, but something told her she was right. Even though it had never happened before, and she had no empirical evidence, she knew.

She hadn't caught a virus, or eaten something disagreeable. Somehow, despite all the care they'd taken, she'd gotten pregnant. The worst wonderful event in her life. As much as she'd wanted a commitment from Trevor, she wanted his baby more. He was an honorable man. She could have both.

But, dear God, at what cost to their perfect friendship?

12

TREVOR'S MOTHER smiled distractedly as he joined her at her regular table at Jean George, the restaurant of choice at the Trump Tower, a casual café where the entrees were smaller, but the prices weren't. Doris had brought the big purse, which sat next to her on the banquette. Inside the purse was a dog, if you could call something that tiny a dog. Caesar was a miniature something-or-other, with long shaggy hair that hid his eyes, and a tiny row of sharp bottom teeth that always made him look like he was smiling. Doris didn't go anywhere without Caesar, and restaurants were no exception. During their meal, she would surreptitiously slip tiny morsels of whatever she was having into the bag. In all the years Trevor had dined with her, he'd never heard that dog make so much as a peep.

"How are you, sweetheart?" Doris said, kissing the air near his cheek.

"Just fine, Mom. How are you?" He settled back, and looked for the waiter, anxious to get his first drink. Lunches with his mother were usually two-drink affairs, but when things got hairy, he'd get three. He hoped it wasn't going to get hairy.

"I'm a little angry at you," she said, frowning at

him with thickly painted pink lips. Doris was as meticulous as ever, with her perfectly overdone makeup, her pink Chanel suit, and the diamonds she never went without. One in each ear, one on a gold chain around her neck. Trevor was convinced she slept in them.

"Why are you angry? I'm a perfect son."

"You are not. You're very mean, and you know it."

He sighed, willing the waiter to come out from hiding. "Just because I can't get excited about your latest boyfriend, doesn't make me mean. It makes me prudent. They come and go with such lightning speed, that if I'm not careful, I'll get whiplash."

"You see? That's just what I'm talking about. You don't even know Didier, and you disparage him right to my face."

"Didier?"

"He's French."

"God, I hope so."

Doris's mouth pursed. "He's also asked me to marry him."

"No. Please, no. Mother, live with the guy if you have to, but don't marry him."

"How can you say that?"

"Because I've watched you do this five times. Or is it six?"

"Didier will be the last."

He shook his head sadly. "You said that about Don. And Gerald. And all the others."

"This time, it's true."

The waiter arrived, and Trevor listened to his mother order the sea-scallop appetizer, a slice of the foie gras, and a martini with two olives. When the young man turned his way, Trevor decided it was too busy on this Friday afternoon to risk losing him again, so he ordered three Manhattans, to be delivered all at once. Also, a club sandwich. He ignored the waiter's sniff and Doris's disapproving glare. A wedding announcement was definitely cause for a three-Manhattan lunch. Unfortunately, at the rate Doris got married, he'd be an alcoholic by the time he turned forty.

"So, when are you going to do the deed?" he asked.

"Next month. We're going to have a small ceremony at my apartment, then we'll go to France. He's got a home there, and he wants me to see it."

"Sounds wonderful," he said. "You've never had a house in Europe before."

She smiled, and he really saw her age. She'd had him young, but her mileage was starting to show. At forty-eight, she still looked good, but the lines by her eyes and her mouth were inescapable proof that being a perennial bride didn't stop the clock.

"Let's see," he said, picking up his water glass, more to have something to hold than because he was thirsty. "There was an apartment in Los Angeles. A townhouse in Las Vegas. And didn't someone have a beach house on Maui?"

"Stop it, please."

"Hey, they're your trophies, not mine."

"I don't think of them as trophies. I think of them as missteps on my road to happiness. Which, thank heavens, I've finally found."

He nodded. It wasn't worth it to argue with her, or even discuss it, for that matter. She'd never see her pattern. Or maybe she did see it, and didn't care. Hey, everyone needed a hobby. Some people collected stamps—Doris collected husbands.

"What do you hear from your father?" she asked, smiling disarmingly as the waiter brought them their drinks. He put Trevor's Manhattans in a neat little row, as pretty as you please.

"I haven't talked to Dad in a couple of months," he said. He picked up number one and gave it a taste. Perfect. Knowing he was armed, he relaxed a little more, stretching out his legs, careful not to hit his mother's.

"That's not surprising," Doris said, her bitterness undisguised, and more familiar than the way she colored her hair.

"I think he's still with Tiffany."

"Tiffany. I ask you, is that any kind of name for a grown woman?"

Trevor almost brought up Didier again, but he took another sip instead.

They didn't speak for a few minutes, and Trevor guessed that Doris was taking a brief trip to her past, when all her troubles started. When his father left her. According to legend, she'd been so deeply hurt that she'd barely made it through alive.

The waiter came back with the food, and before

he'd gone two steps, Doris had picked off a tiny sliver of the liver paté and slipped it into her purse.

"So, are you coming?"

"Pardon?"

"To the wedding."

"I don't know, Mother. It depends."

"On what?"

"On the date. On whether I can stand to listen to those words again. I just don't know."

She inhaled deeply, holding the breath an inordinately long time, then let it out slowly.

"I'll save you the dilemma," she said, her words as brittle as the crackers on her salad plate. "You don't have to come. You don't have to do anything. I'll let you know when I come back from France."

"Mother—"

"All your brothers and sisters will be there, but I'll explain that you were called out of town. They'll believe me."

It would be a considerable crowd, if the whole gang showed up. Doris never picked a guy without several children of his own, and then they weren't content until they made some together. He didn't even know half his stepsiblings.

"I'm sorry," he said. "I'll try to come. I promise."

"Thank you." She nibbled a bit on a scallop. "I don't suppose you've met anyone."

He almost told her, but he caught himself in time. She wouldn't understand his relationship with Lee. She'd wonder why he wasn't going to marry her, if he cared so much about her. What his mother would never understand is that what he had with Lee was far too important to subject it to something as twisted as marriage. "No, Mom. I haven't met anyone."

"It's such a shame," she said. "You can't truly be happy until you get married. Until you give yourself completely to your other half."

He finished Manhattan number one, and started working on number two.

LEE DROPPED her purse on the kitchen table and hurried to the bathroom, clutching the paper bag in her hand. She had to know for sure. This morning, as she'd sat on the edge of the bathtub waiting for her stomach to settle down, she'd thought of a hundred different reasons she couldn't be pregnant. They'd been careful, really careful. She was only two days late, and that happened sometimes, if she was really stressed. Then there was the whole theory of sympathetic pregnancy. Her close friend had talked of little else than morning sickness for three weeks, and, subconsciously, Lee was probably just attempting to share the experience.

She pulled the kit out of the bag and read the directions three times. It seemed simple enough. Pee on a stick. She didn't need a master's degree to do that.

Shaking like crazy, she finally managed to hit what she was supposed to, then she put the stick on the sink while she washed her hands. She kept waiting for it to turn blue. Blue was good. Pink was bad. *Come on, blue.*

What in hell was she going to do if it came out pink? There was no question about having the baby. But there were lots of other questions. What to tell Trevor, for example. And when to tell him. After she saw a doctor? When she started to show? And if she did tell him, what was he going to say? Would it end the relationship? Would he ask her to marry him, for the sake of the child, then resent her for the rest of their lives?

She dried her hands, keeping her eye on the little stick. Who knew five minutes could last this long? Who knew she could survive with her heart hammering so hard in her chest?

She looked away, forcing herself to ignore the stick. A watched pot and all that. It was no use. She had to see. She had to know.

As the seconds ticked by, she hovered, barely blinking, with her fingers crossed. She thought about the irony of it all. How Katy and Ben had tried for months and months with nothing to show for it, and then she and Trevor do the horizontal bop a few times, and bang. She closed her eyes, afraid to look. Counted off the seconds.

Finally, her wait was over. She opened her eyes.

The stick was pink.

She was pregnant. With Trevor's child.

It was already growing inside her. A baby. A real live, honest-to-goodness kid.

She held on to the counter as she eased herself

down to the edge of the tub. Folding her hands neatly in her lap, she tried to remember how to breathe.

This changed everything. Not just her relationship with Trevor, but *everything*. Her job, her apartment, her future. She had no room for a nursery. But how could she afford a two-bedroom in Manhattan? How could she afford a crib? A changing table? Diapers!

She moaned, putting her head in her hands. George meowed as he rubbed her leg, and then Ira had to get in on the act. They always knew when something was wrong, and boy, howdy, was something ever wrong. She was going to be a mother. Trevor was going to be a father. They were going to be *parents!*

The cats calmed her down a bit, and then, unexpectedly, the dread in her stomach turned to something else. Excitement. Not pure, not without fear, but yes, it was excitement.

A baby. A little girl, perhaps. Or a little boy. A little Trevor, suckling at her breast, warm and pink and beautiful. A toddler, full of energy and mischief, learning at the speed of sound. A teenager— Well, that was a little too much to contemplate at the moment.

She stood, amazed her legs held her, and picked up the stick. It was still pink. Just to be really sure, she'd go to the doctor. Sticks were wrong sometimes, right? Just like condoms sometimes didn't work?

Oh, lordy. This was some pickle...with ice cream on top.

TREVOR WAITED impatiently for Lee to answer her phone. He wasn't exactly drunk, but he wasn't exactly sober, either. Lunch with Doris always had that effect on him. She seemed to counterbalance any reaction to alcohol. It was quite a trick, but then his mother had a whole purseful of tricks.

Stepfather number six. As soon as his real father heard about the upcoming nuptials, he'd ask Tiffany to marry him. That's how it always worked in his parents' cockamamie game of lifetime tag. In his family, no marriage went unpunished. No alimony was too great to risk. The person with the most ruined lives in their wake wins.

He pushed the elevator button again, almost dropping his cell phone in the effort, and willed Lee to answer. The little prayer worked.

"Hello?"

"It's me," he said.

"Hi."

"You okay?"

"Yeah, I'm fine."

She didn't sound fine. "Mind if I come over?"

"I don't know, Trevor," she said. "I'm kinda busy."

"I need to see you, kid. I wouldn't ask if it wasn't important."

She didn't answer for a while. Long enough for the elevator to reach the lobby. "Sure," she said, finally. "Come on over."

"Thanks. I'll be right there." He clicked off, then stepped into the elevator. Thirty seconds later, he arrived at her floor, and in a few steps, he was at her door. He knocked, the relief at seeing her, at being with Lee, a physical sensation. His heart slowed, his anxiety eased. He was entering his safe place, the one spot on earth where nothing could harm him: Lee's arms.

She opened the door, and he kissed her before she had a chance to act surprised that he'd arrived so quickly. Kissed her properly. He ran his hand down her back, all the way to that incredible behind of hers, and lifted her into the air, turning her around so he could kick the door shut with his foot. All the while the kiss went on, and he tasted her taste, and he smelled her scent. His worries drained away, and his spirits lifted. It was magic.

Finally, he let her go. She looked so beautiful, staring up at him, blinking like that.

"Where did you call from?"

"Downstairs."

"Why didn't you tell me?"

"I don't know."

"Have you been drinking?"

He nodded. "Yes."

"Oh," she said, her eyebrows raised. "A particularly good vineyard?"

"Not wine at all, my dear. Booze."

"Ahhh."

"I had lunch with Doris."

"Ahhh," she said again, but this time it denoted understanding.

"So you see why I needed to come here."

"Yes," she said, stepping out of his arms. "Can I get you some coffee?"

"No. Yeah. Decaf."

"Why don't you tell me about it?" she suggested, heading toward the kitchen.

He stopped to pet the boys for a moment, then followed her. He was glad he'd caught her off guard. She hadn't had time to fuss over herself. What she didn't realize was that she didn't have to fuss for him. He liked her without makeup, in her old comfy robe, and with her hair piled on top of her head. He even liked her ancient bunny slippers.

"So?" She said, getting out the green Starbucks canister. "Shoot."

"She's at it again," he said, leaning against the refrigerator. The kitchen was small in the real world, but for Manhattan, it was pretty large. Two people could actually be inside at the same time. And, of course, there was no bathtub in here, which was always a plus. "This time, it's some French guy named Didier."

"Didier?"

"Uh-huh."

"What does that make, six?"

"Unless I've miscounted. They're getting hitched next month, here at mom's place, then winging off to his house in France."

"You have to give her some credit," Lee said, as she poured the water into the coffee machine. "At least she picks wealthy men."

He laughed. "She could give lessons."

"Which is not a bad idea," Lee said. "I know they teach flirting at NYU, so why not nabbing a rich husband?"

"I'll mention it to her," he said. "But getting married seems to be a full-time job. I don't think she'll have the time."

Lee smiled, but something about it felt wrong. It didn't get to her eyes. Now that he looked at her, he knew she'd lied when she said she was fine. "You're still sick, aren't you?"

"Me? No, not at all."

But that wasn't the truth because she didn't look at him, and her words were all jumbled together in her rush to spit them out.

"Lee, did you stay home today?"

She shook her head, busying herself with mugs and spoons and artificial sweetener.

He reached over and felt her forehead. No sign of a temperature. But she kind of jerked away from his touch, as if she didn't want him to...

Oh, damn.

His stomach clenched, and all the anxiety he'd left on her doorstep came scrambling back, bringing some friends along for the ride. All of a sudden, he got it. She didn't want him here. She only agreed to see him because he hadn't given her an out.

He knew it, because he recognized the signs. Usually, he was the one going through this little charade—just before he broke it off.

He left the kitchen, and went to her bookshelves, studying the spines blindly as the panic threatened to take the rest of his senses. She didn't want him anymore. No, that wasn't right. She didn't want to be lovers anymore. The friendship was still intact. Of that, he felt sure. Positive. That part wouldn't ever end.

But not sleeping with her? Not feeling that body next to his, naked and warm and beautiful? Not stealing a glance while she slept, so innocent and vulnerable it squeezed his heart until he couldn't breathe?

"Are you going?" she asked.

"I don't want to," he said, before he could stop himself.

"Well, I'm pretty sure your mother will forgive you."

He closed his eyes, realizing his mistake, feeling so stupid. She'd meant the wedding, not her apartment.

Or had she?

He forced himself to look at her again, to watch her as she brought the two steaming mugs to the coffee table. She put them down carefully, then she sat, curling her legs underneath her at the very edge of the couch.

She didn't look at him at all.

She didn't look at him because she didn't know how to tell him, how to break it to him that the experiment had failed. That she wanted them to go back to the way they were.

"Come sit down," she said, patting the seat next to her.

Maybe he'd gotten it wrong. The three Manhattans, his mother. Didier. That was enough to threaten anyone's perception. He headed for the couch, and Lee smiled. Her regular smile. All the way to her eyes.

As soon as he sat, before he got his mug, he turned to her. "I didn't give you much of a choice about my being here," he said, gauging her reaction. "I'll be out of your hair in a minute."

She hesitated. He froze, scared to move a muscle for fear he'd jinx it. Then she shook her head. "Stay," she said, and the welcome in her voice was the best thing he'd ever heard.

He sighed, got his mug, and settled down next to her, banishing his paranoid notions, amazed what three little drinks and a shot of his mother could do.

He'd been worried for nothing. He could pour out his dysfunctional family secrets in complete safety. Lee would listen, then make him feel whole again.

Propping his feet on the coffee table, he began to talk.

13

LEE HAD ALREADY planned what she was going to say. Trevor thought she was under the weather, and she'd use that as her excuse. But she needed to say something now, before he assumed he was welcome to spend the night.

It had been the most difficult evening of her life. He'd talked for two hours, telling her all the reasons his mother was nuts, his father was crazy, and that he'd never, under any circumstances, fall into the marriage trap like his parents.

He'd been so worked up, he hadn't noticed how quiet she'd been. He certainly hadn't caught on that he was breaking her heart. It was terribly difficult not to tell him her news. But until she went to the doctor and got a confirmation, she wasn't going to do that to him. Besides, she needed some time to think. The repercussions flowed like a river; with every bend, a new thought occurred to her. Should she raise a child in Manhattan? She didn't want to live anywhere else. But what about schools? Money for schools? Clothes! It wasn't a river; it was white-water rapids, and she had no paddle.

She wanted to believe it wasn't fair, that it was all his fault somehow. But Trevor wasn't to blame.

She'd known his feelings from day one. He wasn't even to blame for the baby. They'd both been diligent in using condoms, and it wasn't his fault that something had gone wrong. She'd also known long before the pink stick that Trevor would take responsibility for the baby. She'd be able to count on him completely to help her financially. Not just that. He'd be a father to his child. A real father.

The only thing that wasn't "fair" was that she wanted more. She wanted to live with him, as husband and wife. She wanted him to believe that she was different. That not only was she worth marrying, but that not marrying her would kill him.

She wanted to go through the pregnancy with him by her side. To raise this child as a couple, and not from two different apartments.

It was clear now that she'd done irreparable damage to their friendship. It simply wasn't enough anymore. Being his friend would never be enough again.

"You okay?"

She looked down. Trevor had laid himself out on the couch, resting his head in her lap. She'd been running her fingers through his hair, just absently petting him, and she realized she'd stopped mid-stroke. Now he looked up at her, his concern visible even though he was upside down.

This was her moment. All she had to do was say no, that she wasn't okay. That she didn't feel well. But the words were held back by a sudden and incredibly powerful need to be held. All she could manage was a small shake of her head.

He sat up immediately, then moved over so he could take her in his arms. He folded her close and tight, so her head rested on his chest. Now he petted her, stroking her hair, rubbing her back, rocking her like a child.

"What's wrong, honey?" he asked softly.

She couldn't speak. If she did, he'd hear her unshed tears. She shook her head, praying he wouldn't stop giving her the comfort she so desperately needed.

"Is it your stomach?"

She wanted to laugh. Yes, it was her stomach, but no, it wasn't a bug. Everything in her wanted to tell him it was a baby—their baby.

When she didn't answer, he pulled back, lifting her head with a gentle finger under her chin. "Can't you tell me?" he asked.

His gaze captured hers, searching for clues. A foolish part of her hoped he'd guess, hoped he'd see the truth in some magical fashion. Instead, he leaned forward and kissed her. So tenderly, she nearly burst into tears.

She wrapped her arms around his neck, concentrating on his lips, on his kiss. She buried herself in the embrace, afraid to let go for fear of falling apart.

His hand moved from her back to her breast. The sensation was so intense, it took her mind off everything. He let go, and the world came back. She didn't know if it was because of her new condition, or because she felt so desperate, but it didn't matter. If he touched her, and kept touching her, she'd be all right. She couldn't face going to her bed alone.

Dammit, she needed her best friend tonight. And if she couldn't pour her heart out in words, she could do it with her body.

She stood up, taking his hand, and led him past the kitchen, where she shut off the light, then to her bedroom, where she did the same. Normally, they didn't make love in the dark, but tonight, she couldn't let him see. She wasn't a good actress, and he knew her too well.

All she knew was that she needed him next to her, inside her. Now.

She helped him out of his clothes, then as she took her robe and sleep shirt off, he found a condom packet and tore it open. She wanted to tell him not to bother. That it was too late for such things, but she didn't. She climbed into bed, and pulled him down next to her.

"What's going on with you?" he whispered. "What's the rush?"

"Just make love to me," she said. "Now. Right now." She reached down to find him ready, thick and hard and anxious, the thin latex barely a barrier to her inquisitive touch. Her hand moved down his length, and she squeezed him gently, eliciting a moan.

Releasing him, she found his hand and guided his palm down her stomach. He stroked her there, not knowing what was growing inside her, yet exploring as if this part of her was somehow new. His fingers trailed from her belly button to the top of her mons, then back again, caressing her with infinite care and tenderness.

As he dipped lower again, he didn't stop, but let his fingers toy with the soft patch of hair, tugging, but not painfully. Lee closed her eyes, willing herself to focus only on his movements, on the response from her heated body.

When he moved lower still, she stopped trying. She didn't have to. All that existed was the pressure on her swelling flesh, the intimacy of his finger sliding inside her hot folds. She arched her back, spread her legs in invitation, wanting more, wanting them to be as close as two people could possibly be.

Just as she opened her mouth to ask him for what she wanted, he mounted her, holding the bulk of his weight on his strong arms.

She reached down, running her hand quickly over his stomach until she found his erection then guiding him until he touched the outer lips of her sex. She wrapped her legs around his hips, urging him forward.

He wouldn't be rushed.

Slowly, tormenting her with his patience, he entered her, inch by aching inch. Her hands found his back, and she held on as hard as she could. She couldn't stand it. *"Please,"* she begged.

"Please, what?"

"Please, come inside me."

"I am inside," he teased, his voice wicked, his intent clear. He knew what it did to her to have to wait when she was this close, this ready.

"What do you want?" she asked, ready to give him the moon if only he would—

"*You*," he said. More a growl than a word. Possessive, selfish, demanding. "*All of you.*"

"I'm yours," she whispered back, knowing he didn't understand the depth of her pledge. Suffering because it was so heartbreakingly true.

Finally, he couldn't tease any longer. He thrust inside her, filling her with his flesh, making her whole, making her complete.

It wasn't until she felt the trail of tears on her cheeks that she realized she was crying. She squeezed her eyes shut, forcing herself to stop, or at least to wait. She couldn't let him know. Not yet. Not tonight. Tonight, she would be his. Tonight, they would be perfect lovers.

Tomorrow was soon enough to have her world fall apart.

TREVOR LEFT the next morning while Lee was still in the kitchen nursing her coffee. He wasn't happy about leaving, but he had an interview with Francis Ford Coppola about his vineyard. He'd met the director once or twice, but he'd never had a chance to really talk with him, so this opportunity wasn't something he could put off.

But his mind wasn't on wine, or celebrity vintners. Lee hadn't been herself now for two days, and he was very concerned. As he stood on the street corner, lifting his hand to hail a cab, he got out his cellular and hit Katy's speed dial number. She answered on the second ring.

"Have you talked to Lee?" he asked, as soon as the hellos were finished.

"Not today."

"What about yesterday?"

Katy paused. "No, actually, I didn't."

A yellow cab pulled up and Trevor got in. "The Plaza," he said to the cabdriver. Then he settled back on the seat, knowing the ride was going to be a long one in this traffic.

"What's wrong?" Katy asked.

"I don't know. I was hoping you would know. She's just not herself."

"Is she sick?"

"That's what I thought, but she doesn't have a temperature or anything."

"Well, why are you worried then?"

He had to think a minute to put his feelings into words. "She's been really quiet. Moody. And Katy, last night, when we were in bed, she was crying."

"Crying?"

"Not sobbing or anything. But I felt tears."

"Did you ask her why?"

"No. It didn't seem right to ask her."

Again, Katy paused. The cab came to a sudden stop, and he lurched forward, bracing himself with his free hand. A cacophony of horns and curses made hearing impossible. When it settled down, he asked Katy if she'd said anything.

"I said, maybe she's having PMS."

"Maybe," he said. "But I don't think so."

"She's not bitchy, eh?"

He smiled, wondering if Katy would have let him get away with saying the same thing. "No, not at all. Just blue."

"So you're thinking it's about you two, huh?"

"Yeah, I'm heading there. But I don't want that to be it."

"Has she said anything about—"

Trevor waited for her to finish the sentence, but she didn't. "About what?"

"Nothing."

"Katy. Come on."

"No, it's not my place. I'm sorry I even brought it up."

"Don't make me come over there."

"Damn," Katy muttered. "She's gonna kill me if she thinks I said anything."

"I won't tell. Scout's honor."

"It's no big deal. She's just been wondering if, you know, if you and she could, uh..."

"Could what?"

"Could be maybe more than, you know, friends."

"You want to say that again in English this time?"

"More," Katy said, "than friends. More than friends with sex. Get it?"

"You mean boyfriend and girlfriend?" he asked, not even trying to hide the surprise in his voice.

"It happens. It's not like she's asking you for a kidney, for God's sake."

"Uh, yeah. Okay. Well. I guess I was pretty much off the mark."

"Why?"

"I thought she wanted to stop being friends with sex," he said. "I didn't know she wanted more."

"I'm not saying for sure that she does. She didn't exactly tell me that. But I know for a fact she's never going to come out and talk to you about it."

"Why not?"

"Hello?" Katy said, exasperation making her voice rise. "Because you're Trevor, that's why."

"Oh, yeah," he said, understanding exactly what Katy was saying. "So you think that's it, huh?"

"I don't know. I probably shouldn't have said a word."

"I'm glad you did. Honest."

"Trevor?"

"Hm?"

"Anyone seeing the two of you together would already think you're a couple. You spend all your free time with her, right?"

"Right, but we've always done that."

"How do you feel when she's not available? Doesn't it make you feel like something important is missing?"

He shoved aside the memory of last night, when he'd thought for a sickening moment Lee wanted him to leave.

"I thought so," Katy said, breaking his silence. "Now do one more thing. Picture Lee back together with Carl. How do you feel?"

Betrayed. Mortally wounded. Ready to punch Carl's lights out. "I get your point."

"Okay, then. And Trevor? Be careful. Don't rush into anything. Everything will turn out fine."

"I want to believe you."

"Then do."

The cab turned the corner, and Trevor saw the flags flying in front of the Plaza Hotel. He didn't want to do this interview now. Not with so much to think about. "Katy, I have to run. But don't worry. You did the right thing by telling me."

"God, I hope so. Keep me posted."

"You got it." The cab pulled up into the circular drive, and a uniformed bellman opened his door. "I'll talk to you later," he said, then clicked off the phone. He gave the driver too much money, but he didn't care. All he could think about was what Katy had said. And how he'd reacted. What scared him most was that he was starting to think like his mother.

He got out of the cab, and went to the entrance, but he didn't go inside just yet. He stood there, staring at a potted plant, wondering what the hell he'd gotten himself into. They never should have changed things. As great as it had been to make love to her, and that was an understatement, it wasn't worth what it turned him into. An irrational, possessive idiot. He couldn't undo what had happened. but he could go back to being her friend, no perks. Lee would understand. She had to. Because the only thing scarier than hurting her was losing her.

LEE HUNG UP THE PHONE. She'd done something she'd never done before. She'd called in sick. She'd once gone to work while she had walking pneumonia, but today, even though her stomach wasn't giving her much trouble, she couldn't face the phones, or the board or the other brokers. She needed to be alone.

It was almost nine, and she still hadn't gotten out of her sleep shirt. The debate now was whether to crawl back in bed, or take a bath first.

The bath won. She put her empty coffee cup in the kitchen sink, then made her way into the bathroom. It took her a few minutes to decide which of her many scented beads she was in the mood for, but she finally settled on lilac, one of her favorites.

She turned on the faucet, adjusted the temperature and poured in several beads. The scent hit her quickly, seeping into her along with the steam, relaxing her instantly.

She got up and closed the door, deeply insulting George and Ira who would whimper until she came out again. Then she took off her robe and her sleep shirt, letting her gaze move to the mirror. Her stomach was still flat—well, not Cindy Crawford flat, but there was certainly no hint of what was happening inside her.

It was all going to change. Her stomach would grow, her breasts would get big and heavy. She'd get stretch marks, and then after she had the baby, she might lose the weight, but she'd never have *this* body again. Of course, she planned on taking the pregnant aerobics classes at her gym, but she'd talked to enough people to know that for mortal women like her, some changes were inevitable. Madonna might be able to have a baby and still pose nude, but for Lee, the possibility of a *Playboy* layout was frankly out the window.

She smiled. Yeah, right. Like they were pounding on her door now.

Glad to see she still had something of a sense of humor, she climbed into the tub, sighing as the hot water eased her weary soul. For a long time, she didn't do much, just soaked while she took deep, lilac breaths. If she thought at all, it was about relaxing the muscles that came to her awareness, until she felt as limp as a cooked noodle.

The only sound she heard was the soft scratching at the door, where George and Ira waited impatiently.

Their child.

The thought came whole, fully formed, as if she'd given birth to her future right there, lying in the water. She could see it all somehow, in a flash of insight that startled her just as it made all the sense in the world.

She would have the baby, of course. She would love it and raise it the best way she knew how. It wasn't a mistake at all, she realized. It was a gift. Something she hadn't even known she wanted.

The baby was *theirs*. Why that came to her so profoundly, she didn't know, but it was the truth. Nothing that happened for the rest of her life would change that fact. She and Trevor had created a life together, born out of a love so strong it defied description.

It wasn't the kind of love she'd heard about in storybooks and in movies, but that didn't diminish it one iota. So what if they didn't marry? If they lived in separate apartments? The child wouldn't be loved any less. In fact, she couldn't think of a baby in the world who would have a better father.

This little one would be surrounded by love. By her aunts Katy and Susan, and her uncles Peter and Ben. And she or he would have a best friend the same age, to play with and grow with and to complain about parents with.

Lee wasn't alone, either, although it suddenly hit her hard how much she wished her mother were still alive. How much she wanted to talk to her about this incredible event. But Lee had the feeling her mother knew that she was taken care of. That she'd built a family, a strong one.

Tomorrow, she'd see the doctor. And once her pregnancy was confirmed, she'd tell Trevor. She wasn't worried about his reaction anymore. It would take him a while to adjust, just like it was taking time for her, but he'd come around.

She'd never tell him that she'd fallen completely, utterly, head over heels in love with him. Because she knew that Trevor cared for her so much, that the damn fool would ask her to marry him, and that was the only thing in the whole scenario that would be wrong.

And in return for that kindness, she'd have their baby. As far as she could see, it was a pretty damn good deal.

All she had to do was stop wishing for what she couldn't have, and be grateful for what she already possessed.

14

THE INTERVIEW had gone surprisingly well. The surprise wasn't that Francis was fascinating—that was a given—but he'd been remarkably perceptive, guessing that Trevor had been preoccupied, and not only that, but that his preoccupation was about a woman.

How he'd known, Trevor didn't have a clue, but it was a fact. At lunch, while drinking some of the best wine Trevor had tasted in a long time, he'd confessed that he was completely mystified by women and marriage. Francis had talked to him for a long time, mostly about how lucky a man could be to find the right woman. How it made all the difference. The same life experiences might happen to a man, married or not, but when he was alone, it was all in black and white. It was a woman's perception and interpretation that gave things color.

Now, half an hour later, Trevor couldn't get that image out of his mind. He hadn't gone straight home, preferring to walk in the park for a while. It was a nice day, sunny, but not hot. Nothing beat spring in Manhattan. The trees were alive with birds, the sky a remarkable blue, considering it was the city. Some part of his mind registered the joggers and the in-line skaters, the couples walking hand in hand, and even the children dashing dangerously through the thick of things. But mostly, he thought about Lee.

She'd played such a pivotal role for so many years, it was hard for him to remember his life before her. As he walked slowly down the winding paths, his memories took him a fair piece further. Before Lee, he'd never liked the telephone. It had never occurred to him to use it for anything other than logistics. But her first phone call had changed that. They'd talked for over two hours. Lee carried the conversation, of course. He hadn't learned the art yet. Although he couldn't remember what they'd said, he did remember how often he'd laughed, how astute her observations were and how she had a completely different take on things from his own.

They'd lived in the same dorm, and knew a lot of the same people, but once Lee started talking about them, the people he'd blindly passed in the hall became three-dimensional. She showed him their quirks, their foibles, and from then on, when he met up with the guy from across the hall, he saw him as Phil, who wore the same football jersey every day, and wondered if he ever washed it.

All these years, Lee had been his color commentator, turning the game of life into something fascinating. Confusing him a hell of a lot, but also making him think. She'd added depth and scope, and it was her influence, he now realized, that had made him a good writer. Because he didn't just write about wine, but about people. Their quirks, their foibles. Things he'd never have noticed if Lee hadn't shown him the way.

Katy's words came back to him, and he felt the need to sit down on an empty park bench. Lee wanted more. He still wasn't sure exactly what that meant. Living together? Marriage? He couldn't give her what she wanted.

As well as she knew him, didn't she understand that it wasn't a matter of choice, but a matter of biology? All he had to do was look at his family to see that marriage wasn't his destiny, not if he wanted to remain sane. It wasn't just his parents, although anyone could see that if genetics had any truth to it at all, he was doomed. Further proof, in the form of his brother, sealed the deal. Tom, although only twenty-two, was already on his second marriage.

And because Trevor was nothing if not practical, he'd decided to break the chain. To end the foolishness. *To take the coward's way out.*

The thought kicked the air from his lungs. He struggled to find solace in the old excuses, but it was no good. The truth was too big, too powerful.

It wasn't rotten destiny that kept him from committing to Lee, or concern that he would break her heart. It was terror that she would break *his*. He loved her, not as a friend, but as a soul mate. On some deep level, he'd known that for years. If they married and he blew it... He shuddered. He wouldn't survive. Better to save the friendship while he still could. Admit their noble, if foolhardy, experiment had failed. He'd back off gradually. Tonight, for example, he wouldn't go over there. She wasn't feeling well, anyway. It was for the best. She'd hardly miss him.

He'd miss her, though. The thought of his bed, so empty, so cold, made him want to stay up all night. Or at least fall asleep on the couch. But she'd think something was funny if he didn't call her.

He got out his phone, intending to dial her number. Instead, he put it back, got up and headed out of the park.

"This is a surprise. Come in."

Trevor smiled, relieved that he was welcome. He went inside, heading for the couch.

"To what do I owe this honor?"

"I need to talk."

"Fair enough. About what?"

"Lee."

Susan nodded. "Let's get comfy, shall we?"

He sat down on her white leather couch, amazed as always at Susan's apartment. It was huge, pre-World War II, and had three bedrooms. The decor was pure Susan, classy and modern with a few surprises here and there, like the framed animation cells she had lining the hallway.

She walked back into the living room carrying a bottle of white wine and two glasses. "You want this?" she asked.

He shook his head. "Just came from a tasting. Water would be good, though."

She turned around and went back into the kitchen, and he had a moment to think about how beautiful she was, even when she had no makeup, and wore faded jeans and a T-shirt. Then she came back, still carrying the wine, but also a glass of water for him. After handing him the drink, she settled down across from him in a matching white leather chair, curling her legs underneath her, and placing her wine on the coffee table. "What's up?" she asked.

"I need some advice."

"And you came to me?" she asked, her surprise genuine.

"Well, sure. You've known Lee and me for a long time. You've been through some trials of your own. I figured you'd be the one to talk to."

"Trials, huh? Interesting way of putting it." She poured herself a glass of chardonnay, then settled back into position. "Shoot."

"I don't know how much you know. It's impossible to keep up with all of you, but according to Katy, Lee isn't happy."

"Go on."

"Evidently, despite the original agreement, she wants more."

"More of what?"

"I'm not sure," he said. "But I think it means she wants a commitment."

"Ah," Susan said, nodding as if he'd just given her the last piece of a puzzle he couldn't even see.

"I don't know." He took a big drink of water, and although it slaked his thirst, it didn't make his thoughts any clearer. "I'm not sure what to do."

"That's interesting, coming from you," she said.

"Yeah." Especially since thirty minutes ago, he'd decided to back off. "If it was anyone but Lee..."

"But it is Lee."

"Yep."

Susan leaned forward a bit, her expression serious and intent. "Do you think you could do it? I mean, for the long haul? Through sickness and in health and all of it?"

"That's the question, isn't it? I've never believed I could."

"But you think with Lee there might be a chance?"

He wanted to believe it so badly his teeth ached. But he just shrugged. "Maybe."

She leaned back, studied him for a while, then looked at her hands. Finally, her gaze came back to him. "All I can do is tell you what I think. It could be completely wrong, though, so you have to take it with a grain of salt."

He nodded.

"I think you need to trust your instincts. The big risk here is losing her for good, am I right?"

"Yeah," he said, just hearing her say the words making him sick to his stomach.

"As long as I've known you, you've never seen yourself as a marrying kind of man. Whether you are or not isn't as important as what you believe you are. Because I think we create it. All of it. With our attitudes and beliefs, even if we don't understand them. Even if they bring only pain."

"So by believing I'll never make it in a marriage, I'll make it come true?"

She nodded. "It's a real shame, though. I think you and Lee make an incredible couple. That if things had been just a little bit different, you could have had it all."

"Like Ben and Katy?"

"Like Ben and Katy."

His longing was so strong he couldn't breathe, couldn't speak. Like a penniless kid with his nose pressed to the candy store window, he wished a miracle would fill his empty emotional pockets. "You don't think I can change the way I believe, huh?"

"Maybe. Maybe if you love her enough, you can. But I won't lie. I've never seen anyone change something so fundamental about themselves. Not that it can't happen," she added, obviously sensing his disappointment.

"The risk is pretty big."

"Yeah. The reward could be pretty big, too." For an instant her nose was pressed to the candy store window, too.

In the sympathetic silence, Trevor weighed the pros and cons. "I don't want to give her up," he said at last.

"You don't have to."

"But I can't keep sleeping with her. That'll only make things worse, right?"

"Trevor, why don't you *ask* her?"

He almost dropped the water glass, but made a quick recovery. "Ask her? About this?"

Susan nodded. "She knows you better than anyone."

"Sure, but—"

"Trust her. She's your friend, first."

He put his glass on the table, then rested his elbows on his knees, staring straight down to the plush white carpet beneath his feet. He thought about talking to Lee about this. What a minefield that conversation would be. One false step, and kaboom, his most treasured friend could be gone in a flash.

He looked up again, catching Susan in an unguarded moment, the pain and sadness on her face so clear, so present, it made his own heart ache. Then it was gone, and she looked cool and calm once more. But he'd seen the truth. The kind of pain only losing someone you love can bring.

Panic drove him to his feet. "Thanks, kiddo. I'll let you get back to your regularly scheduled life now."

"Oh, joy," she said dryly. "Another night of television. Yahoo."

He went over to her and bent down to kiss her cheek. Then he took her free hand in his, and brought it up to his lips. He kissed her there, too. "You take care of yourself, okay?"

She nodded. "I always do."

LEE LEFT the doctor's office, moving with the flow of the busy lunchtime foot traffic, but not really paying attention to where she was going. The shock of the doctor's words still reverberated through her body, centering on the small life that was unequivocally growing inside her. No more doubts, no more hedging her bets. This was real.

She had to tell Trevor. It was as much his reality as her own, and he deserved to be a participant from the beginning. Not on the phone, though. She needed to see his reaction, even though she already had a good idea what it would be.

He'd undoubtedly ask her about marriage, but she was prepared. He'd never know what was in her heart and feel forced to do the traditionally expected "right thing." After a while, she felt sure she'd learn to accept that it had to be this way. And the ache that had begun at the moment of her decision would ease in time. She'd be preoccupied, busy gestating as she prepared for the next phase of her life. Surely, she'd have no time for regrets. Right?

She turned onto Lexington Avenue, then got her cellular phone from her purse. As she dialed Trevor's number, she noticed that half the people walking by her were talking on the phone. What an odd phenomenon. The phone rang several times, but it was his machine that answered, not him. After his brief message, she said, "Call me. I'd like to see you tonight, okay? Bye." Then she called her own machine, and the first message told her she needn't have tendered the invitation. Trevor's voice, kind of echoey and distant, told her that he was on his way to California, to the Napa Valley where he was going to finish his article. He'd be back next week. Hope she felt better. Click.

Dammit. She shoved the antenna down a little too forcefully, then had to unbend the slim wire before she could slip the phone into her purse. It seemed odd that he'd gone to California without telling her. They'd seen each other just the other night, and had spoken on the phone yesterday. It wasn't like him.

Normally, she knew his schedule, at least the big picture, a week or two in advance.

Some opportunity must have popped up from his interview, that's all. It wasn't about her, and it wasn't about them. Just work.

But now she was really in a jam. She couldn't tell the rest of the gang, not before she told him. Which was going to make things quite horrible, as she was constitutionally incapable of keeping a secret for longer than twenty minutes.

Maybe she could just tell Katy. No. No, it wouldn't be fair. Trevor had a right to be first.

Stepping to the curb, she signaled a cab. Although her mind was elsewhere, she still had to work for a living. Tonight, she'd lay low. Maybe not even answer the phone. She planned on stopping at the bookstore on her way home and picking up a pregnancy primer. That would keep her busy.

It was a good plan, one that would have worked, except for the knock on her door at seven-thirty. After reading about the expense of having a child, she fervently hoped it was going to be Ed McMahon and the prize patrol, but it turned out to be Peter.

"Is this okay?" he asked. "Are you busy?"

She shook her head, gesturing him inside. "No rehearsal tonight?"

"Nope. The director and the diva both have the flu. At least, that's what they claim. Personally, I think they're having a lovers' spat. Either that, or they're running off to get married."

"Sounds complicated."

Peter flopped on her couch, smiling as George and

Ira came to welcome him. "It's theater," he said. "It's always complicated."

She smiled as she headed for the kitchen. "What can I get you?"

"You have any Yoo-Hoos?"

"But, of course, my dear." She didn't like the chocolate drink herself, but she always kept a few in the fridge in case Peter stopped by. He was addicted to the stuff. "What's up?"

"I had to tell someone," he said. "I couldn't hold it in any longer."

He sounded so excited that Lee hurried back, handing him his drink and perching on the edge of her chair. Even without his enthusiastic words she could see something big was going on. His hair was rumpled, as if he'd forgotten to comb it this morning, and his handsome face was flushed, as if he'd run all the way here.

"It's Andy."

"Yes?"

He filled his lungs with air, then let it all out in one big whoosh. "I know this sounds crazy, and I know it's happened really fast, but Lee, he's the one."

She grinned, feeling his happiness as if by osmosis. In all the years she'd known Peter, he'd never been like this. No one had ever been "the one," not even Jude.

"I didn't expect it at all," he said, standing up, his energy clearly too powerful for him to keep still. "I'd liked him back in college, but it wasn't enough to stop the presses or anything." He went behind the couch, to the bookcase, scanning the titles, but not really seeing them, she guessed, just giving his eyes something to do. Then he turned back to her, his smile making her laugh out loud.

"So, what changed?" she asked.

"Everything. Him, me. All I know for sure is that this is it. I've never felt anything like it. Sort of calm, you know? Like I've gone back home."

"You don't seem calm to me."

"That's just because I got it today. About two hours ago, to be precise. I'd been having this great time, and I wanted to be with him every minute. We talk and talk, and he's this normal guy, except he's not ordinary at all. He loves his computers, but not to the geek extreme. Just passionate." Peter put his hands on the back of her couch and leaned forward, looking as if he were going to do a quick dozen push-ups. "But it's how I feel when I'm with him that's really the miracle."

"Tell me."

He hesitated for a few seconds, as if searching for the right words. "He gets me. Not just the cute, charming parts, but the ugly, obnoxious parts, too. And he loves them all. Seriously. He doesn't care that I'm completely obsessed about acting, or that I'm an idiot when it comes to my checkbook." He pushed himself off the couch, and circled it again, resuming his seat across from her. "I feel whole," he said. "Go on, shoot me for being clichéd, but dammit, Lee, it's the truth."

She understood. More than she could tell him. More than she cared to admit to herself. "I'm so glad for you," she said, feeling the first heat of tears warming her eyes. "You deserve this."

He grabbed her hands, squeezing them between his. "You know what? I agree. Although sometimes I have to pinch myself to make sure this is real."

"Oh, Peter. I'm so glad you told me. This is incredible."

"Yeah. Man, I never thought I'd find what Ben and Katy have. But I was wrong."

"I'm getting chills," she said, and it was true. She was beyond thrilled for Peter, who'd gone through more than his share of bad relationships. Of all her friends, he was the sweetest, the most trusting. Which of course made him an easy target.

"We're moving in together," he said. "This weekend. He's giving up his place. We're going to try it at my apartment for a while, then see if we can find something a little bigger."

"Oh, that's wonderful. We'll have to have a big dinner to celebrate."

Peter nodded. Then his animation ebbed, and his smile faded. "So, what's going on with you and Trev?"

She made sure not to change her expression. "Nothing. He's away for a week in California."

"Are you still doing the boinking experiment?"

She nodded. "At least we were. I'm not so sure it's going to continue."

"Why not?"

"It may not be theater, but it's complicated."

He sighed, squeezed her hands again. "Does he know you're in love with him?"

She tried to pull back, but Peter held her steady. "What do you mean?"

"It's obvious, honey. We've all known, but wanted you to tell us first. I saw you at the wedding, and at the Sunday brunches. You've got it bad. I just hope Trevor can get his head out of his butt long enough to see what he's got. You two need each other."

"You're mistaken," she said, finally pulling her hands free, shifting her gaze from his probing stare. "We're just friends, remember? Friends with sex."

"I may be an actor, but I'm not stupid. And I'm not blind. It might have started out as friends, but it's become something else. So don't blow it. This love thing, it's all it's cracked up to be. Trust me."

She smiled, but it wasn't with joy. "It takes two to have a love thing, Peter. Two people who want the same thing."

"He does, you know. But you have to remember he's a guy, and sometimes they're not too bright. Give him some more time. He'll get it eventually."

"I love you, Peter, but you're wrong. He'll never make a permanent commitment to any woman. That's the *last* thing he wants in our relationship."

"Are you sure?"

She found his gaze again, because this time she could look at him with complete authority. "I'm sure. It's about the only thing in the world I am sure about."

Peter sighed. "Then I'm sorry. Really. For both of you."

"Yeah," she said. "Me, too."

She didn't call or send him a birthday card, but he'd
let it slide. After all, it was almost his own fault.
    He went and unzipped the side pocket on his suit-
case, dug out the flattened, rolled-up dollar bills. He
counted out twenty, then twenty more, put his hand
into the zipper pocket once more, but it came up
empty. Twenty-four dollars.

15

TREVOR TURNED ON his computer, and as he waited
for it to boot up, he checked his Day Runner. Yep, today was Lee's birthday. Not that he'd had to look.
He remembered her birthday all right. She wouldn't
let him forget.

    Every Christmas she gave him two new calendars,
one for his Day Runner and one of those little stand-
up jobs with all the *Far Side* cartoons. But before she
wrapped them, she went to her birthday and colored
the page, filling it with little hearts and exclamation
points, then in big bold letters that covered most everything she wrote, "The Celebration Of Lee's
Birth!"

    But then, that was Lee, subtle as a freight train. It
made him smile, as so many of her nutty stunts did.
He thought about the present he'd gotten her in California. She wasn't easy to buy for, and he hoped she
liked what he'd picked out.

    He got up and went to his suitcase, still packed
even though he'd gotten home four hours ago, and
got out the small box. After a lengthy conversation
with a very nice woman at the jewelry store, he'd finally settled on a cat pin. It reminded him of George
and Ira, except this cat had diamond eyes. Lee would

get a kick out of it, and he was pretty sure she'd wear it. If not, he had the receipt in his briefcase.

He took the wrapped present back to his desk, then slipped the floppy disk into his machine. He'd written his article, and then some, on his trip. Not out of any great surge of ambition, but because he'd needed a distraction.

It hadn't worked, of course. He'd thought about her constantly. The worst was at night, in the cold, sterile bed of the hotel room. He hadn't just missed making love to her, he'd missed talking to her, hearing about her day. He'd missed being able to look up and see her in one of her silly sleep shirts, with her hair all wild, and her clean beautiful face.

The week had been difficult. He'd waffled so many times, he needed syrup. There was a lot to be said for going back to the way things had been, before that dinner when Lee had told him her scheme. He'd been comfortable, and he'd felt safe knowing she'd always be there for him. Uncomplicated. Familiar. Easy. All the things he'd come to take for granted after eight years.

His decision final, he went to the phone. Lee always got to pick the restaurant on her birthday.

SHE COULDN'T SIT STILL. Trevor was due any second, and her nerves were about shot. She'd have loved a drink, but that was out of the question. Tonight was the night. She was going to tell him about the baby. It seemed appropriate somehow that it was her birthday. A suitably dramatic ambience for news that was going to rock his world.

She went to the kitchen to feed the cats, but saw their bowls were not only full, but both George and Ira were chowing down.

Where was he?

According to her Felix the Cat clock, whose tail wagged and eyes moved each second, Trevor was going to be late if he didn't get here in the next five minutes.

The kitchen was no good. She walked back to the living room. God, it was clean. She'd been on a Martha Stewart kick for the past week, and not only was the apartment sparkling, but she'd brought in fresh flowers, candles, bought matching pillows for the couch, put out bowls of homemade potpourri and lined her drawers. In other words, she'd nested, tucking in a feather here and a twig there. It was so predictable, it made her nauseous.

If she turned into one of *those* mothers, she'd shoot herself. The kind who teach their children French while they're still in the womb. Who send video résumés to preschool admissions officers. Who live their lives through their child so single-mindedly, that when the kid finally leaves, there's nothing left but an empty Mommy suit.

She wouldn't do that. Not to little Gwyneth or Dallas. No, scratch Dallas. Maybe Max. That was a good, solid name. He'd grow up strong and steady, a guy to be counted on. Yeah, Max.

She headed for the bathroom, flipped on the light, and picked up her hairbrush. She didn't need to brush her hair, but at least it gave her something to do with her hands. But she didn't. Instead, she laughed at her own reflection. At the care she'd taken with her makeup. The long burgundy dress she'd bought that afternoon. The perfect droopy earrings she'd found at the thrift shop on Seventh.

For a woman who was about to tell the father of her unborn child that she was perfectly content with raising said child alone, she was awfully dressed up. She'd taken just as much care with her underwear, which didn't make a whole lot of sense since she wasn't planning on sleeping with him. Ever again. Ever.

She sighed, put down her brush, and headed back to the living room. Halfway there, he knocked.

Her heart went into fourth gear, skipping second and third altogether. Suddenly, her throat went dry. Her hands got clammy. She couldn't move.

He knocked again, and she forced herself forward, pasting a pleasant, nonpanic-filled smile on her face. Then she opened the door.

Oh, dammit. Trevor wore the exact same pasted-on grin. He was going to tell her something awful. She just knew it. Like he'd met someone in California and would she like to come to the wedding. It had to be that. Wasn't it always that?

"Can I come in?" he asked.

She stepped back, nodding. He paused, then kissed her very lightly on the cheek.

Double dammit. She'd been an idiot. A complete fool! How could she have believed, even for a minute, that she could give him up without falling apart? That she'd be stoic and brave and mature, when all she felt was a need for him so strong it could knock

Manhattan into the sea? And here he'd given her a friend kiss. Not even a friend-with-sex kiss. Certainly not a darling-marry-me-right-now kiss.

"Happy birthday!"

She swung the door shut, so hard it made them both jump. "Thanks."

"I've missed you," he said, moving toward the couch. He didn't seem to notice the clean carpet or the new pillows. Or that she was dying a tiny little death. That in the past few seconds, all her good ideas and rational thoughts had vanished like smoke.

"How was your trip?" she asked, not ready yet to look at him. As he settled down on the couch, she headed for the kitchen, almost shaking with her realization. What was she supposed to do now?

"It was good. I got a lot done. Finished the piece and gathered enough material for several more."

"Great," she said. "What can I get you?"

"What? No champagne?"

She'd forgotten. It was always champagne on her birthday. "I figured you were probably sick of wine after your trip. How about soda?"

"Sure," he said, after a confused pause. "Soda's good."

While she got out the glasses, filled them with ice, and poured the Sprite, she scrambled to find something to hold on to, some way of facing the evening without going completely crazy.

Of course, she still had to tell him the news, but she'd do that later, after she'd calmed down. It wasn't supposed to happen this way!

"Peter came by the other day," she said, deciding right then that they needed hors d'oeuvres. She finished pouring the drinks, then went back to the fridge, hoping that somehow she'd stashed a nice platter of shrimp cocktail next to the jar of mayonnaise. Unfortunately, it was still her fridge, and the best she could come up with was some celery and cream cheese. It would do. At least it would keep her busy.

"So, how is he?"

She had to think a second to remember she'd brought up Peter's name. "He's great. He's in love."

"No kidding?"

"He says this is the one."

"I assume he means Andy?"

"Yep. They're moving in together."

"Well, I'll be," Trevor said, and his voice sounded kind of funny. But she had no time to worry about that, not while she was busy spreading the Philly on the celery sticks, and searching desperately for her equilibrium. The best thing to do was relax. Breathe deeply. Think calming thoughts.

"I hope it works out for him," Trevor said. "It sure is tricky."

"What, living together?"

"No, love."

She spread her thumb with a nice dollop of cheese. "Right, right. Very true."

"It can get confusing."

"Uh-huh."

She wiped her hands on a towel, then put all their

refreshments on a tray. She didn't shake too much when she headed for the living room.

Trevor sat with his arms on the back of the couch, and his legs crossed comfortably. But that wasn't what made her almost drop the tray. The ring box on his knee did that.

A ring box. It had to be. Earrings or a necklace would be in a different shape. What else looked like a ring box but a ring box?

"Happy birthday, Lee."

She smiled again, then put everything down on the coffee table. He was hard to read. She couldn't gauge his mood at all, which never happened. She knew this man better than anyone in the world, but right now, she didn't have a single clue as to what he was thinking.

The enigmatic grin was still in place. He didn't appear nervous, and yet he didn't look her in the eyes, either.

"Don't you want to open it?"

"Of course," she said, her voice too loud and cheery. She sat next to him, but then her nerve left her. He had to hand her the box.

She opened it carefully, not ripping the wrapping to shreds with her usual fervor. Her hands shook, and she hoped he didn't notice.

It was a ring box. A black ring box. With a thudding heart and a silent prayer, she opened it.

At the exact second Trevor saw disappointment change her face, he understood what he'd done. She'd thought it was a ring. The box... Of course, she'd thought the cat pin that had reminded him of Ira and George was a ring. Oh, God.

"It's lovely," she said, very softly. But he heard the choked emotion, saw her blink several times, then she shifted on the couch, putting her dignity back on like a coat.

What had he done? Why had he not seen it? He'd hurt the one person he loved most in the world. He cursed himself for his own stupidity, and then another thought occurred. What if he'd *wanted* her to think it was a ring? What if he'd wanted this exact reaction as proof that if he asked her to be his wife, she'd accept?

The thought blinded him for a moment, making it hard to think. Good God, the way she looked when she'd opened the box, trembling with anticipation. She wanted it to be a ring. She wanted them to be together forever, and it hit him like a ton of bricks that he was in love with her, and that he wanted to be with her for the rest of his life. Lee was the key. She'd opened the door to the candy store and invited him in. It was as simple as that.

"Lee," he said, leaning forward, trying to slow his fevered thoughts. To make absolutely sure she understood.

She rose abruptly, still holding the box in her hand. "Excuse me," she said, "I have to—"

She didn't finish the sentence, just rushed away from him in a blur of burgundy.

"Wait." He bounded from the couch, but she was too quick for him. She made it to the bathroom, and shut the door in his face.

"Lee, come out."

"I'll be out in a minute," she said.

"No, you don't understand."

"Yes, I do. I understand completely."

He opened the bathroom door. She stood by the sink, holding the end of a long string of toilet paper up to her eyes. Stepping back, she almost stumbled over the commode.

"No, you don't understand," he said. "I gave you the wrong box."

"What?"

"The pin. I got it all wrong. I need it back."

"What are you talking about?"

He moved forward, grabbed her shoulders and steered her backward so she could sit on the edge of the tub. Once she was settled, he lowered the lid on the toilet, and sat down, too. She still held the paper, only now she was twisting it in her fingers.

"Here's the thing," he said. "I didn't get it until now, see. I thought I had a handle on this, but I was wrong."

She sniffed, but didn't stop him.

"This, this experiment, it didn't go the way I thought it would. I had no idea...I didn't know I'd ever feel this way."

"What way is that?" she whispered.

"Like I want...more."

"More?"

He nodded, wishing like hell he knew how to tell her, what to say. "I love you," he said.

"And I love you."

"No, you don't understand. I *love* you."

"You love me?"

He nodded again. "Like Ben and Katy."

Her eyes grew huge and dark. Where was her happiness? Her blinding smile?

"It's a really big risk," he forged on. "I know the odds aren't in our favor."

"It's just that—" He took her hand in his and squeezed, the feel of her so right he regained his confidence. "...for the first time in my life, I feel lucky, not doomed. Other people aren't us. Other women aren't you. My God, I've been so blind, focusing on what could happen instead of what did happen. Lee, adding sex to our friendship made the earth move, but we stood strong, didn't we? We didn't break apart. In all the years I swore I'd never get married, never have kids, I left out a big part of the equation...."

Lee opened her mouth, but nothing came out except a strange little, "Oh?"

"Trust," he said. "I left out trust. The kind that best friends share. The kind you and I have had since that night we had pizza. And when we're old and tired and rocking on the porch, watching our grandchildren playing in the yard, our trust will still be strong. Almost as strong as our love."

The tears began to fall, inching their way down her perfect face. He made a soothing sound, reached for a piece of tissue, but then he used his thumb instead. Once he touched her, he couldn't stop. He smoothed her hair, massaged her nape, cupped her cheek. She pressed against his palm like a cat seeking a chin scratch.

"I want us to get married," he said. "And, don't faint or anything, but I want us to have kids."

She sat bolt upright. And finally, *there* was the happiness in her eyes. The blinding smile that warmed his heart as nothing else in the world could. "Are you sure?" she asked, as if afraid he might say no.

In answer, he leaned over the last few inches, and kissed her. Softly, at first, but the taste of her salty tears moved him to stand, pulling her up with him. He held her tight in his arms, kissing her as if it would save his life.

Lee ran her hands over his back, testing, making sure he was real, and this was real and that she hadn't gone crazy with wanting him.

The taste of him, wintergreen with a hint of coffee, convinced her. The scent of him, so masculine even his soap couldn't hide it. And especially the feel of him. She knew it was true. And so good, it made all other good things feel ashamed.

After a long time, she pulled back and looked at him with clear eyes and a steady pulse. There was still one more thing to talk about.

"What?" he asked.

"Don't get me wrong," she said. "This truly is the most romantic thing in the history of the world, but I was thinking maybe we should continue in the other room."

He laughed, kissed her again, then took her hand and led her out of the bathroom and into the bedroom. They sat on the edge of the bed, knees touching, hands entwined. "There's something else," she said.

"Do I need to worry?"

She shook her head. "God, I hope not."

"Why doesn't that reassure me?"

She drew in a deep breath and took the plunge. "Remember that upset stomach I had about a week ago?"

He nodded, his eyebrows coming down in confusion. "Sure."

"Well, it wasn't an upset stomach."

Concern joined the confusion on his face. "Did you go to a doctor?"

"Trevor, I'm pregnant."

The news hit him slowly, in stages. First his eyebrows went up. Then his face paled about a shade and a half. His jaw dropped, leaving his mouth open. His gaze traveled down her body, pausing to stare at the general vicinity of her stomach, then climbed back up again.

"Are you okay?" she asked, her spirits sinking.

And then he smiled. A broad, thrilling, heart-stopping grin that told her everything she needed to know.

"We're going to have a baby?"

She nodded. "In about eight months."

"But didn't we..."

"Yes, we did. Go figure."

"Holy cow."

"Yeah."

He blinked a few times, then kind of shrugged. "Well, shoot. I guess we should get married soon."

She felt the last bit of tension leave her chest. "I guess we should."

"A baby?" he repeated, breaking into a goofy grin.

"Our baby."

"This was some experiment," he said.

She nodded.

"There's only one thing I was wondering."

"What's that?"

"Why aren't we having sex?"

The words that had started it all.

She smiled intimately and leaned forward. "Because we're going to be too busy making love." Just as her lips touched his, her phone rang. She ignored it, knowing it was Katy, or Ben, or Susan, or Peter. Knowing she'd tell them all, but not tonight.   Then the phone in his jacket started ringing too.

"Hold that thought," he ordered, snatching her phone and walking both annoying contraptions out of the bedroom. A moment later he was back, closing the door. "Now, where were we?"

She smiled with all the happiness she'd ever known, all the faith she'd ever held, all the love there ever was. "I believe we were just at the beginning."

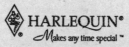

If you enjoyed what you just read,
then we've got an offer you can't resist!

Take 2 bestselling love stories FREE!

Plus get a FREE surprise gift!

Come escape with Harlequin's new
Series Sampler

Four great full-length Harlequin novels bound together in one fabulous volume and at an unbelievable price.

Be transported back in time with a Harlequin Historical® novel, get caught up in a mystery with Intrigue®, be tempted by a hot, sizzling romance with Harlequin Temptation®, or just enjoy a down-home all-American read with American Romance®.

You won't be able to put this collection down!

On sale February 2000 at your favorite retail outlet.

HARLEQUIN®
Makes any time special ™

Visit us at www.romance.net

PHESC

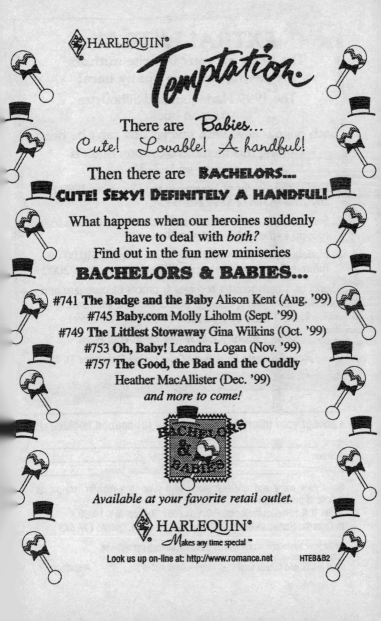

EXTRA! EXTRA!

The book all your favorite authors are raving about is finally here!

The 1999 Harlequin and Silhouette coupon book.

Each page is alive with savings that can't be beat!

Getting this incredible coupon book is as easy as 1, 2, 3.

1. During the months of November and December 1999 buy any 2 Harlequin or Silhouette books.

2. Send us your name, address and 2 proofs of purchase (cash receipt) to the address below.

3. Harlequin will send you a coupon book worth $10.00 off future purchases of Harlequin or Silhouette books in 2000.

Send us 3 cash register receipts as proofs of purchase and we will send you 2 coupon books worth a total saving of $20.00 (limit of 2 coupon books per customer).

Saving money has never been this easy.

Please allow 4-6 weeks for delivery. Offer expires December 31, 1999.

I accept your offer! Please send me (a) coupon booklet(s):

Name: _____

Address: _____ City: _____

State/Prov.: _____ Zip/Postal Code: _____

Send your name and address, along with your cash register receipts as proofs of purchase, to:

In the U.S.: Harlequin Books, P.O. Box 9057, Buffalo, N.Y. 14269

In Canada: Harlequin Books, P.O. Box 622, Fort Erie, Ontario L2A 5X3

Order your books and accept this coupon offer through our web site
http://www.romance.net
Valid in U.S. and Canada only.

PHQ4994R